GW00585034

Also available from Headline

The *Invasion: Earth* Companion *by Peter Haining*

Invasion: Earth – The Last Echo

Peter Cave

From the series created by Jed Mercurio

HEADLINE

First published in paperback in 1998
by HEADLINE BOOK PUBLISHING

10 9 8 7 6 5 4 3 2

ISBN 0 7472 6001 X

Typeset by
Letterpart Limited, Reigate, Surrey

Printed and bound in Great Britain by
Clays Ltd, St Ives plc

HEADLINE BOOK PUBLISHING
A division of Hodder Headline PLC
338 Euston Road
London NW1 3BH

Invasion: Earth –
The Last Echo

PROLOGUE

The third, and final wave of German bombers was gone now, droning eastwards down the Thames estuary like a swarm of monstrous hornets. What had been a savage roar faded to an angry buzz and was eventually swallowed by the tumultuous sounds of the devastation they had left behind them. The crackle of flames, the regular blasts of oil drums and paint canisters still exploding like delayed-action bombs, the all-pervading wail of 'Moaning Minnie' as the air-raid siren changed its wavering pitch to the single, continuous tone of the all clear.

It was 11.15 p.m. on July 14, 1944. It should have been dark, but the glow of fires from London's burning docklands lit up the night sky as brightly as any dawn. Great gouts of flame and oily black smoke erupted from both sides of the Thames, both within the sprawling clusters of wharves and warehouses along Surrey and East India Docks and beyond, from the streets and homes of the city's beleaguered East Enders from Bermondsey to Whitechapel, East Ham to Bow.

Lieutenant Charles Terrell picked his way gingerly between the piles of smouldering debris, mindful of the current rumour that the Luftwaffe were now dropping anti-personnel mines in the wake of their main bombloads. It was probably untrue, the rational part of his mind realised. There were new rumours practically every day – borne either of malice by German sympathisers or from the genuine confusion and bewilderment of innocent civilians caught up in a horror they could not possibly understand. They ranged from feasible stories of paratrooping Nazi spies and saboteurs to wild and fanciful tales of new chemical superweapons which could turn even the most loyal British subject into a fanatical agent of the Third Reich. Plausible or not, they all had their effect, as witnessed by his own faltering footsteps.

Terrell pulled himself up with a conscious effort. It was all part of the war, he told himself. As much a part of the psychological attack on the civilian population as the constant, mindless bombing and the poisonous propaganda spewed out nightly by the likes of Lord Haw Haw and his traitorous cohorts.

Terrell stopped in his tracks, taking time to draw in a long deep breath of smoke-laden air and exhale it in a deep, reflective sigh. A dozen feet to his left, Private Grover also came to an abrupt halt, camouflaging his immediate concern beneath a nervous grin.

'What's up, Lieutenant? Found something?'

Terrell shook his head, his own face impassive. It was a gesture which somehow managed to convey a total and absolute sense of weariness, bordering on despair. 'No, just thinking, that's all. Just looking.' His quietly modulated, cultured voice sounded oddly out of place after the broad cockney twang of his subordinate.

Any immediate threat of danger over, at least for the present, Private Grover's grin broadened. 'Blimey, sir – they don't pay us to think, y'know. Can't have people *thinking* in the British Army.'

The joke failed to lift Terrell's spirits. He continued to stare, grim-faced, at the devastation all around him. Something in the rubble slightly ahead and off to the right caught his eye. He stepped towards it, muttering under his breath as he moved, more to himself than for Grover's benefit.

'My God, this is a savage bloody war.'

Keeping pace with him, Grover let out a slightly bitter laugh. 'Well, at least we're giving the jerries back as good as we get. If you think this place looks a mess, just imagine what our boys are doing to Berlin and Munich.'

Terrell stopped again, looking down at the grisly sight which had caught his attention. 'Yes, that's exactly what I mean,' he murmured. 'All those cities, all that beautiful architecture . . . all these innocent people.'

Grover could see it too, now, and could not fail to be moved, even though he should have become used to such sights. It was a body, or what was left of one. A young woman, probably no more than twenty-one or twenty-two. Somebody's daughter. Somebody's sweetheart. Now she was no more than a butchered piece of dead meat. Both legs were missing, along with one arm. On the arm which remained attached to the torso, the white armband of the WVS was clearly visible.

Grover was shocked to silence, but only for a moment. Terrell's last comment demanded some sort of riposte. He spoke with the wounded air of an affronted patriot. 'Blimey, sir – you sound as though you're feeling sorry for them. We're fighting a war, remember?'

Terrell shook his head again. His eyes had a distant, faintly vacant look. 'We're not *fighting* this damned war, Private. We're just swept up in it, blown along like so many seeds of grass in a whirlwind.' He looked down at the dead girl again. 'Here's who's fighting this war, Grover. People like her. Women, children, babies . . . the innocents.'

Grover was silent, not knowing what to say. He didn't understand Terrell, but the depth of conviction in the man's voice was overpowering. He began to wander away, shaking his head in confusion. He was an odd one, was Lieutenant Terrell. Deep, mysterious, unpredictable. Too complicated.

Terrell was relieved. He needed to be alone with his own turbulent thoughts, perhaps try to make some sense of them. If anything could be made to make sense after everything which had happened. He wasn't even sure of that any more.

It had all seemed very simple back at Cambridge in 1938 in the rarefied world of academics and optimistic young graduates. The world was a beautiful place, filled with the potential to be made even better. Science, art and technology were booming as the mid-century approached. War had ended for all time in the bloodsoaked trenches of Ypres and the Somme. The future was exciting.

Only the existence of a demented little Austrian painter had cast a shadow over this utopian dream. And Terrell, along with the bulk of his idealistic young contemporaries, had flocked to the recruiting offices to join up, ready to fight against tyranny and oppression, and all those other grandiose concepts which had seemed to mean so much.

Now, after four long years of one of the most savage conflicts in human history, they weren't even concepts any more. Just words – the meaning of which Terrell found himself struggling to redefine.

A shout from Sergeant Lynch, the third member of the squad, cut through his waking nightmare.

'Lieutenant, over here, quick. I've found something weird.'

The urgency of Lynch's tone snapped Terrell back into action. He broke into a run, the fear of anti-personnel mines suddenly forgotten.

Lynch was standing by the partially demolished wall of a warehouse, strewn with collapsed, charred timbers and beams. Above the debris, something gleaming and metallic jutted out, arcing up into the night sky.

'What the hell *is* that?' Lynch demanded as Terrell reached him.

There was no immediate reply. It was not a question Terrell could answer. He edged around the corner of the shattered building until he could get a clearer view.

Grover had arrived to join them. He let out a little whoop of excitement. 'Christ, it's a bleedin' doodlebug. A whole one, what ain't gone off. The boys back at the War Ministry'll probably give us a medal for finding one of these little beauties.'

Lynch was not convinced. 'Don't look like a V-1 to me,' he muttered dubiously. 'Don't look like a V-nothing.'

Terrell said nothing, but continued to study the object with an increasing sense of wonderment, studying its clean, sleek lines, the polished perfection of its dark, metallic surface. He was finding it hard to accept that the thing was any kind of a bomb at all. There was a kind of aloof, even unwordly beauty about it, he had decided. He found himself wondering who could possibly have designed and crafted such a thing, imagining it to be a labour of love. Surely not the work of some fanatical Nazi scientist, cold-blooded and cold-hearted.

Both Grover and Lynch were seeking reassurance from their superior. As Grover had pointed out, it wasn't in a British soldier's brief to be required to think for themselves. Faced with something unknown, they turned to Terrell.

'Well, what do you think it is, sir?' Lynch asked.

'More to the point, what do we *do* with it?' Grover wanted to know.

Their questions concentrated Terrell's attention on the problem to hand. He was, after all, in charge of a bomb disposal team. The first thing to do, obviously, was to determine whether it was a bomb or not. He became businesslike, snapping out his orders.

'Lynch – check out the business end, see if you can see any sign of a warhead of any sort. Only easy does it, man. Grover – nip back and find the nearest working 'phone. We're going to need an M.o.D. team in here. And an ambulance – there may be casualties.'

The two soldiers accepted their orders with curt nods – Lynch's one of trepidation, Grover's one of agreement. Terrell began to skirt around the object for a different viewing angle as Lynch crept in closer.

It was *so* beautiful. The air immediately above it had a slightly shimmering quality, denoting a quite considerable heat source. Wisps of a darkish vapour still emanated from it, appearing an unearthly orange colour in the glow of the continuing fires all around. Terrell found himself thinking of the early chapters of the H. G. Wells novel, *War of the Worlds*. A faint shiver ran through his body. Once again, it took Lynch's voice to snap him out of his reverie.

'Christ, sir – there's something alive inside this thing. I can hear movement . . . and a sort of whimpering sound.'

'Stand back, Sergeant.' Terrell's voice was coldly authoritative, that of an officer taking control. He moved in quickly towards the mid-section of the strange craft as Lynch backed away from it. Quickly – but not quickly enough. For the rest of his life, Charles Terrell would curse himself for what happened next.

A hatch in the side of the craft seemed to burst open, seamlessly and soundlessly. One second the structure appeared solid and unbroken, the next there was a large, oval-shaped hole. And something was coming out of it.

Still a good ten feet away, Terrell saw Lynch's hand drop to the Webley strapped to his hip, fumbling with the holster clip. He opened his mouth to scream – 'No' – but it was too late. Lynch had the gun free, aiming and firing in one smooth movement. There was the sound of a single shot, a thin, high-pitched squeal of a creature in pain and then the craft's occupant was tumbling forwards a few feet in front of the open hatch to lay motionless on the ground.

Reaching the spot, Terrell looked down in horror. The figure was small, too small for an adult. It was about the size of a ten-year-old child,

Terrell estimated – but a curiously deformed child. The head, even allowing for the opaque, glass-like helmet which encased it, was far too large in proportion to the rest of the unnaturally thin and stretched-looking body. It was as if someone had taken a human body and tortured it on a rack until it was mangled into a grotesque parody of itself.

Terrell dropped to his knees by the body, probing it gently for any signs of life. There were none. He ran his fingers over the shiny surface of the one-piece garment encasing the corpse, encountering another mystery. It was distinctly warm to the touch and although it felt like fabric, it looked like metal. It was like no other flying suit that Terrell had ever encountered, and he'd seen more than his fair share of crashed planes and dead pilots, both Allied and German.

Finally, he reached the small, dark-stained hole where Lynch's bullet had penetrated the suit and encountered a warm, moist stickiness. Rubbing it between his fingers and the ball of the thumb, he brought his hand up closer to his eyes.

There was no mistaking the texture of blood – but this was unnaturally dark, almost black. As if this was the final clue, Terrell suddenly *knew*, without the faintest shadow of a doubt, that the creature was not human and that the strange craft had come from somewhere a long, long way further than across the English Channel.

Hands trembling, he undid its helmet.

'My God . . .'

Terrell was mute with pity and shock. The creature's head was roughly egg-shaped, with a domed, bulbous and utterly hairless cranium surmounting a thin and high cheekboned face. The eyes, huge and black, were set deep into the skull. Its skin, dry and leathery looking, was the pallid colour of wood ash, but covered in dark, irregular-shaped blotches.

It looked so peaceful and unthreatening.

Terrell rose slowly to his feet, his dark eyes twin pools of horrified sadness. 'You killed it,' he muttered in disbelief. 'You killed it.'

Lynch was defensive. 'I thought he was coming at me, sir. He just appeared out of nowhere.'

Terrell held out his hand. 'Give me your fire-arm, Sergeant.'

Lynch hesitated.

'Do it – *now*! That's a direct order.' Terrell's tone was uncharacteristically sharp.

Meekly, Lynch handed over the Webley. Terrell snapped on the safety catch and slipped it down the front of his tunic. The two men stood looking at each other in silence for a long while.

The silence was finally broken by a faint scrabbling sound from inside the craft. Then another figure emerged, stumbling through the open hatch and falling into the debris. Lynch, facing it, was the first to speak.

'My God, sir – there's another one. And it's still alive.'

Terrell scrambled over to the wounded creature, fussing over it like a mother hen with a new chick. It looked so vulnerable, he thought, so – *gentle*. It appeared terrified, although whether this was due to fear or pain, Terrell couldn't even guess.

'What the hell is it?' said Lynch.

'Wounded, Sergeant,' snapped Terrell. 'It's wounded. Get a stretcher.'

As Lynch moved away, Terrell leaned in towards the creature's helmet. 'Please, don't be frightened. I want to help, if I can,' he murmured softly, hoping that even if it couldn't understand him, the mere tone of his voice would help. There was no response.

Finally, the ambulance and squad Grover had requested from HQ arrived. Two men made their way across the rubble to where Terrell tended the injured creature.

'Major Alex Friedkin, Army Intelligence,' said the first officer. 'A paradox, I know,' he added apologetically.

Terrell straightened up, facing his superior. 'Lieutenant Charles Terrell, sir. Bomb disposal.'

'Your orders are to hand these prisoners over to us now, Terrell. This is no job for bomb disposal.'

Terrell looked away. 'One's dead, the other is severely wounded. He needs urgent medical attention.'

The doctor came across and bent over the patient. He reached for the creature's helmet, looking for a release catch.

Terrell clutched at his arm. 'No, wait!' he urged. 'Our air might be poisonous to it.'

Friedkin and the doctor regarded him as though he was an imbecile.

'Let the man do his job, Terrell,' said Friedkin.

'Sir, I don't believe these people are German! What crashed here isn't a V-rocket,' cried Terrell.

Friedkin let out an exasperated sigh. 'Stand back, Terrell. That's an order.' He silenced the objection about to rise to Terrell's lips with a baleful stare. 'Carry on, doctor.'

Terrell bit his lip nervously as the Army medic struggled with the creature's helmet. It came loose at last with a faint hiss of equalising pressure. Opening the face plate, the doctor pulled it free. His face was at once a strange mixture of shock, horror and pity. He stared at his strange patient in utter silence for several moments.

The doctor found his voice at last. 'My God,' he breathed. 'I've never seen such a constellation of deformities in one human being before.'

Terrell was looking over his shoulder. 'It isn't a human being,' he said, quietly but confidently. 'Surely you can see that?'

For just a moment, doubt flickered across the doctor's face. Then cold logic clicked into place. 'You're talking nonsense, man,' he snapped, testily. 'You'll find every one of these inborn disfigurements in the standard medical textbooks.'

'Most likely the poor wretch is some imbecile plucked from one of the Nazi labour camps to try out this new V-weapon,' Friedkin put in. 'Or the result of some inhuman medical experiment.'

Terrell let out a disbelieving laugh. 'You seriously believe that the Luftwaffe would use feeble-minded freaks of nature to pilot a top-secret experimental aircraft?'

'Well of course they weren't *pilots*, man,' argued Friedkin. 'Just deadweight to test whether this new V-rocket is capable of carrying a crew. Perhaps to guide the weapon to a specific target. Suicide bombers of somesuch. We all know the Nazis are fanatical enough to consider such a thing.'

Terrell was openly dubious. 'Then why not simply use deadweight, sir? And my men have already confirmed that the craft was not carrying any sort of a warhead.'

Major Friedkin hesitated. He was running out of unconvincing explanations and he knew it. In truth, he didn't know what to make of it all.

Terrell seized his advantage. 'Two men, both with the same deformities, identical down to the smallest feature, flying a rocket vastly more sophisticated than any vehicle—'

'Enough, Terrell, enough.' Friedkin was no fool. He could see how – how *unearthly* the thing looked. But . . . 'The priority is to establish whether this is the work of a power of threat to the British Isles in particular and the Allies in general. It's out of my hands.'

'Then let me help, sir,' suggested Terrell. 'Before the war, I was a don up at Cambridge,' he ventured.

A brief smile flickered across Friedkin's lips.

'Why doesn't that surprise me?'

'The point is, sir – I studied anthropology. I really feel I could be of help in this matter. With respect, sir, but Military Intelligence probably doesn't boast all that many men with my qualifications.'

Friedkin was thoughtful for a few seconds. 'Look, I'll do what I can,' he promised finally. 'I'll make representations on your – on *our* behalf with the powers that be.'

Terrell figured it was the best he was going to get. 'Thank you, sir, that's all I ask,' he murmured politely.

A full week passed in which Terrell fretted, without hearing a word. Then the telegram arrived, terse and to the point.

Temporary assignment to special duties. Report to Bickhampton railway station 14.40 hours.

The jeep turned in at the tall wrought-iron gates of a high-walled estate and up a long gravel drive. Terrell gazed at the black, squat shape of a huge and largely featureless building. Everything about the grey-stoned building, from its spartan frontage to its small, barred windows, shrieked of Victorian institutionalism. He had little doubt that it had once served as a bedlam house, and possibly still did.

Friedkin was waiting for him at the front door with a white-coated medic whose uniform bore the insignia of Lieutenant Colonel.

'Seems like the top brass thought you might

have something to contribute after all,' Friedkin said chattily. 'Have to admit I welcome it personally. This whole business has all my people completely baffled, I'm afraid.'

The interior of the building was made up of a series of long, austere corridors with a number of locked and barred doors on each side. It was as forbidding as the façade.

'You've learned nothing, then?' Terrell asked, as the three of them began to walk to the background sounds of muffled, anguished moans and cries of pain.

Friedkin shook his head. 'Interrogation has proved futile. The Germans deny any knowledge, but that's hardly surprising.'

'No, not surprising at all,' Terrell agreed, but Major Friedkin missed the irony in his voice.

'You understand this is a purely temporary secondment?' he said, apologetically. 'It probably won't even appear on your service record.'

Terrell nodded distractedly. He was beginning to find the grim atmosphere of the sanatorium quite distressing. They were just passing a nurse walking hand-in-hand with a young man with Down's syndrome. Terrell could see that his suit was of the highest quality cloth and cut. His features were set into a mask of permanent and absolute resignation.

'What sort of a place is this?' he asked Friedkin.

The Major frowned. 'One you should count yourself privileged to know about,' he muttered. 'This is where the high and mighty lock away their "accidents of nature", if you understand my meaning. I believe it's even had some royal guests in the past.'

Friedkin might have said more, but an admonishing glance from the doctor cut him short. He fell into silence.

Terrell changed the subject. 'And our visitor? How is he?' The term 'visitor' was his own choice. 'Alien' seemed such a difficult word.

Friedkin looked embarrassed. 'He seems to have made at least a partial recovery from his original injuries,' he said quietly. He slowed his pace, allowing the doctor to get a few paces ahead of them and dropped his voice to a whisper for Terrell's benefit. 'To tell the truth, they don't let me see him very much,' he confided. 'Perhaps you'll have better luck.'

The doctor had reached a locked and barred door, guarded by two armed squaddies. He began to open it. Terrell seized the opportunity to speak to him directly for the first time.

'What became of the other one – the dead one?'

The doctor answered curtly, not bothering to look round. 'Standard post-mortem, from which we learned nothing. The remains were cremated.' He pushed the door open and stepped inside.

Terrell followed him, entering what was more like a prison cell than a room. Other than an iron bunk with a thin mattress on top, it was devoid of furniture. The concrete floor was completely bare, without even a strip of linoleum to break up its drabness. The only natural light came from a single, small barred window set high in the wall almost at ceiling level. Beneath it lay the naked and shivering body of the visitor, huddled up foetus-like in the small oblong of sunlight and warmth which it admitted.

Terrell was appalled. Completely forgetting rank and protocol for the moment, he turned on the Army doctor with unusual vehemence. 'What are you thinking of, man? Can't anyone see how cold he is? At least he ought to be given some blankets.'

There was no answer. Disgusted, Terrell took matters into his own hands. He ran back to the door, calling up the corridor to the young nurse with the Down's patient. 'Nurse – would you be so good as to bring some blankets in here, please.'

He returned to the cell, completely ignoring the Army medic and Friedkin and knelt down beside the contorted body of the visitor. It cringed instinctively, pulling itself into an even tighter defensive knot. Terrell noticed discoloured areas around its mouth and cheekbones which looked suspiciously like bruising and suspected that someone had tried to beat it into talking. He spoke quietly, soothingly.

'It's all right. I shan't hurt you. I promise.'

The visitor's huge dark eyes regarded him mutely, fearfully. The poor creature must be absolutely terrified, Terrell realised. He renewed his efforts to comfort it.

'Do you remember me? My name is Charles

Terrell – Charles. I really mean you no harm, I solemnly promise you.'

There was still no response. Terrell reached underneath the visitor and scooped up its frail body in his arms. Too weak and frightened to resist, it allowed itself to be carried over to the bunk, where Terrell laid it down as gently as possible.

The nurse arrived in the doorway, holding a thick pile of blankets. She froze in her tracks, letting out a stifled gasp of shock as she saw the latest 'patient' for the first time.

Terrell spoke without looking up at her. 'It's all right, he won't hurt you. Please, come in.' He tucked the visitor into a comfortable position on the mattress, then turned to reach for a pair of blankets.

The nurse had recovered from her initial shock. Her training and sense of vocation rose to the fore, overriding her fears. She approached the side of the bunk cautiously.

'I didn't know, sir,' she apologised to Terrell. 'The soldiers warned us to stay away from this room. They only let the Army nurses in.'

Terrell treated her to a thin, but reassuring smile. 'It's all right. They'll let you in from now on, I promise.' He cast a challenging glance at the Army doctor, seeking confirmation of this statement and receiving a curt, reluctant nod in return.

Emboldened by this response, he pushed his cause further. 'Please, could we be left alone for a while? I'd like to build up a rapport with our visitor, if I can.'

Friedkin and the doctor exchanged uncertain glances. Finally, in mutual confusion, they withdrew to the corridor outside.

Terrell lifted off the top two blankets and laid them over the visitor's trembling body. It appeared to take immediate comfort from the warmth. Gratified, Terrell turned his attention to the nurse.

'He'll remember you now as the one who brought the blankets. It would probably be comforting for him if you looked after him from now on – would that be all right?'

The nurse nodded. 'Yes, sir.'

Terrell smiled again. 'There's no need to call me "sir",' he murmured. 'My name is Charles.'

'Louise. Louise Reynolds.' She paused, nodding at the visitor. 'And what's our friend called?'

With a wry smile, Terrell shook his head. 'I'm afraid I don't know, and perhaps I wouldn't even be able to pronounce it if I did.'

Louise regarded him blankly, not understanding.

'All I am sure about is that he is someone quite different from the other residents here,' Terrell went on. 'And I believe that he has come to us for a very important reason.' He paused, briefly. 'And with your help, I intend to find out what that reason is.'

Major Friedkin had only heard of General

Marcus Ramsey by reputation, but it was enough to put him on his guard. You didn't get to be Commander-in-Chief of Army Intelligence without cracking a few heads together – even in wartime.

His Whitehall office reflected his status. The room was positively spacious while other personnel were being crammed like sardines into what were little more than oversized broom cupboards. Shown into the great man's presence, Friedkin was woefully aware that his progress report was a negative one, and his tone was suitably apologetic. He cleared his throat nervously.

'So far I'm afraid that we've failed to trace any of the rocket's components or superstructure to any existing manufacturers,' he started. 'But then we don't know if the Germans have opened up factories in the occupied countries, so we're at a distinct disadvantage.'

Ramsey dismissed this information with a faint, and mildly disapproving grunt. 'But we are sure that it *is* of German origin?'

Friedkin tried to be positive. 'That's the assumption,' he said, choosing his words carefully. 'Our own engineers assure us that the design is far beyond anything which the Allies could come up with at the present time.' He broke off for an awkward pause. 'And then, of course, there remains the vexed question of the occupants.'

General Ramsey lifted one grizzled eyebrow. 'Vexed? How so?'

Friedkin shifted his feet awkwardly. 'Our medics are still puzzled by the creature's strange physiology,' he admitted.

Ramsey frowned. 'Creature, Major Friedkin?' he queried, picking up on the single unfortunate word. 'I thought it had been decided that the *prisoner* was the end product of some ghastly medical experiments.'

He had made a mistake, Friedkin realised. General Ramsey was a pragmatist. He couldn't help wondering what the man would make of Terrell. He covered his tracks with an apologetic smile. 'Yes, quite so, General. That is the consensus of opinion.'

But it was too late. The damage was already done. General Ramsey rose from his desk, his face darkening. 'I want you to know, Friedkin, that I'm far from happy with some of these wild stories I've been hearing. Men from Mars, beings from another world, et cetera.' He reached down to his desk and picked up a sheaf of papers, waving them in the air. 'God only knows I have enough crazy stories on my hands at the moment with these. Eyewitness reports of people being abducted by strange forces, never to be seen again.'

Friedkin was intrigued. 'People, sir? What sort of people?'

General Ramsey grumbled testily. 'All sorts. An engineer, a group of fishermen, a gamekeeper, a farmer. Each disappearance seems to follow a pattern – surrounding objects appear to bend, the victim folds away into invisibility and a smell of burning is left behind. And always near water – coastlines, rivers, reservoirs.'

Repeating the string of strange occurrences seemed to make the General even more edgy. He changed the subject abruptly.

'I'm told you have some fool Lieutenant studying the prisoner. Has he managed to communicate yet?'

'With respect, sir,' Friedkin replied, 'Lieutenant Terrell is a very bright young officer. He taught anthropology at Cambridge.'

Ramsey was not impressed. 'And you've left the prisoner alone in his hands? Are idiot officers suddenly in short supply?'

Major Friedkin masked a smile. 'Oh no, sir. I assure you that idiot officers remain a limitless resource of the British Army,' he said, straight-faced. 'Perhaps if you came down and saw for yourself, sir,' he suggested.

The General grunted again – although whether it was in agreement or not, Friedkin was unable to tell.

Terrell had managed to wring a few concessions from the sanatorium staff. A small desk, some pencils and sheets of paper and a soft mattress laid out beneath the window. Discreet night-time surveillance had established that the visitor preferred to sleep on the floor, for some reason. A vase of flowers provided a splash of welcome, if slightly incongruous colour against the overall drabness, as did the educational posters and astronomical charts now stuck around the walls. There was also a carafe of fresh water, from which Louise gave her new patient frequent sips.

Drawings of mathematical symbols and simple cartoons of human physiology littered the floor, discarded by Terrell when the visitor had failed to make any response to them. Despite all these setbacks, however, he persevered.

Eagerly, he displayed his latest drawing – a basic representation of the solar system. Spreading it out on the desk, he jabbed a finger into his own chest and then down at the floor. 'Here, Earth,' he explained patiently, moving to the drawing and indicating the third planet around the sun. 'Earth.'

The visitor regarded him blankly. Terrell pointed to the shaft of sunlight streaming in through the window. 'Sun,' he said, indicating it on the map.

Momentarily, a flicker of understanding crossed the deep, black and fathomless pools which were the visitor's eyes. Encouraged, Terrell repeated the mime in sequence. 'Me – here – home – Earth – sun.' He pointed at the visitor, then indicated each of the planets in turn. 'You . . . where?'

The response was unexpected. The visitor edged back along its bunk, pressing itself tightly into the corner of the walls.

'He's afraid,' Louise blurted out. 'There's something about our solar system which frightens him.'

It had been Terrell's first thought as well, but now he wasn't so sure. He shook his head slowly. 'No, I don't think so,' he murmured. 'I think he's trying to tell us that he comes from somewhere far, far outside our solar system altogether. So far, in fact, that we probably can't even imagine, let alone hope to measure it in our terms.'

He seized a fresh piece of paper and a pencil from the desk, pushing it into the visitor's hands. 'You,' he said gently, pointing again. 'Where?' He gestured upwards to the sun once more.

Terrell felt a mounting sense of excitement as the visitor began to make marks on the paper. It was the first positive response he had seen. He waited patiently until the drawing was finished and took it back. His heart surged. The pictograph was crude, shaky and lacking all sense of normal proportion – but it was unmistakably a representation of a planetary system. Four satellites, in figure-of-eight orbits around twin suns.

It was a moment of breakthrough – but Terrell's euphoria was short-lived. The door swung open unexpectedly with a loud creak. Major Friedkin, accompanied by General Ramsey, stepped into the room.

The visitor cowered in fear at the sudden intrusion. Terrell, instinctively, snapped to attention.

'As you were, Terrell,' Friedkin muttered. He indicated Ramsey. 'This is General Ramsey, Lieutenant. He's come down especially to get a first-hand progress report.'

Major Friedkin made a half-hearted attempt to make it sound as though an honour was being bestowed upon him, Terrell thought, although it didn't feel like it. He nodded deferentially to the General. 'Sir.'

Ramsey glowered at Louise. 'Would you mind waiting outside, Nurse.' It was an order, not a request. He waited until she had left the room before transferring his attention back to Terrell. Terrell noted that he seemed to be deliberately avoiding looking directly at the visitor.

'So, what have you learned?' Ramsey demanded, coming straight to the point.

'I've been unable to establish verbal communication. Clearly their language is very different from ours. That's why I'd like to have a philologist posted here.'

Ramsey frowned. 'A what?'

'Philologist, sir – an expert in comparative language. Perhaps then we shall be able to embark on a study of the visitor's culture and biology.' Terrell broke off to pick up the visitor's drawing. 'However, we appear to be making some small progress in non-verbal communication. I have here a pictograph which I find really quite exciting.'

Terrell might as well have been talking to himself. General Ramsey made it abundantly clear that he wasn't interested in an abstract doodle.

'What I meant was, what have you learned about their military intent?' he demanded.

Terrell was utterly floored for a few seconds. Then he recovered himself.

'Sir, our visitor himself was unarmed and has at no time demonstrated the slightest propensity for violence. His craft was equally without weapons. I believe them to be a totally peace-loving people.'

General Ramsey's lips curled into a sneer. 'I believe several of our leading politicians believed much the same about Herr Hitler at one stage. Now unless it has escaped your notice, Terrell, this country is at war – against a nation which has the capacity to rain rocket-bombs on our capital city.' He paused to glance over at the cowering visitor for the first time. 'So if this freak knows nothing about the project which transported him here, that's because he's not only monstrously deformed but also a congenital imbecile. You have one week to provide us with some answers, then you return to bomb disposal. Do I make myself clear, Lieutenant Terrell?'

Terrell hung his head. 'Yes, General. Perfectly.'

With a loud snort, Ramsey stormed out, leaving Major Friedkin to console the deflated Terrell as best he could. 'Our friend looks much healthier, Charles,' he said gently. 'So you seem to be achieving something.'

Terrell merely nodded glumly. There was so much more that needed to be said, but it seemed useless. Not only was he dealing with military minds, he was dealing with military minds obsessed with war.

That seemed to be about the extent of Major Friedkin's input. With an awkward, half-apologetic smile, he turned to leave the room.

Desperate, Terrell clutched at the sleeve of his tunic.

'Sir, I beg of you. It's absolutely paramount that I have time to establish communication. There may be others here . . . other ships. Who knows what might be achieved if we were able to make contact, establish cultural exchange. Perhaps I could even return with them, as some sort of diplomat. Learn from them and let them learn about mankind from me.'

Friedkin was temporarily overcome by the depth of Terrell's emotion and the sacrifice he seemed willing to make. He gaped at him open-mouthed. 'You'd do that?'

Terrell nodded. 'Yes, sir. I would regard it as the ultimate service not only to my country, but to my world.'

Friedkin was silent for a long time. When he finally spoke, there was a catch in his voice. 'I'm truly sorry, Charles. But General Ramsey seems to have made up his mind and there's nothing I can do. The best service you can do your country is to forget you ever saw this creature.'

'Forget, Major?' Terrell echoed bitterly. 'Forget that it made a journey over unimaginable distances to make contact with us, perhaps to bring us the most important message in our history?'

Friedkin sighed. 'You really do believe that

they came from another world, don't you, Charles?'

Terrell's eyes blazed with conviction. 'Yes sir, I do. And I also believe that the timing of this visit was no coincidence. The major powers of this world are at war, bombing and destroying hundreds of years of civilisation and culture which went before. To an outside observer, it must look as though we are a species hell-bent on self-destruction.'

'And you think they came to help?'

Terrell shrugged hopelessly. 'Perhaps. Or perhaps they were just terrified, seeing that the Germans have developed rockets which might one day be capable of journeying out into space, carrying a creature who appears to understand little else but the pursuit of war and bloodshed. Fraternisation with beings from another earth is the most important moment in our history – it might even be the salvation of a world at war with itself. And look how we've squandered his moment, how we've treated this gentle being.' Terrell stopped, trembling with emotion.

Friedkin drew in a long, slow, reflective breath. 'You paint a bleak picture of mankind, Charles.'

Terrell shook his head, sadly. 'No sir. We paint it ourselves.'

There was nothing more to say. Deeply troubled, doubting himself and everything he had stood for, Friedkin withdrew, shaking his head distractedly.

It was only early autumn, but there was already a marked chill in the night air. Terrell and Louise strolled in the sanatorium grounds, making casual conversation rather than have to face the reality of his imminent departure.

'It's very peaceful here,' Terrell said quietly. 'You're very fortunate to be away from all the bombing.'

Louise nodded. 'I have relations in London. The air raids must be terrifying.' She stopped suddenly, looking up at him. 'Do you have family there?'

Terrell shook his head sadly. 'My father passed away when I was still quite young. My mother lives in Hampshire.'

'But you must have close friends in London.'

A guarded, wistful smile. 'Not really, no.'

'No young lady?'

'No.'

They began walking again. Ahead of them, a nurse was perambulating one of the inmates round in a wheelchair. Although she was warmly dressed up in a woollen shawl, the patient wore only a thin shirt. He was coughing fitfully.

'I can't understand why they keep them out so late,' Terrell remarked. 'The night's so cold and damp.'

A thin, bitter smile crossed Louise's lips. 'Dear Charles. You really are such an innocent, aren't you?' She paused, choosing her words carefully. 'This is a home for incurables. No one ever leaves. They lock people away to make believe they don't exist. I don't know if you can understand, Charles, how fearful people can be of what's different.'

Terrell nodded. 'I understand, most particularly.'

Louise nodded over to the inmate in the wheelchair. 'The staff do that when the family says so. They say it's the kindest thing, but of course it isn't really. They bring them out in all weathers. First a cough, then pneumonia . . .' Her voice tailed off. There was no need to finish. Terrell understood.

'Let's go back inside,' he muttered. 'I'd like to say goodbye to our friend before I leave.'

The visitor sat listlessly on the edge of his bunk, his thin arms and legs dangling over the side. He regarded Terrell as mutely as ever, but Terrell imagined he could feel empathy flowing between them. Perhaps it could sense that its one and only friend in this strange and terrifying place was about to leave, he thought. He spoke slowly, softly.

'I can't even begin to imagine how it must feel, to be so lonely and far from home, so remote from your own kind. But there must have been a reason which brought you here – something that made sense to *you* to travel all this way.'

He fell silent, desperately wishing as never before that the visitor would speak to him. Even now, it might still not be too late. But the creature's pallid lips remained motionless, its eyes revealing nothing but a deep, dark emptiness.

Terrell sighed deeply. 'You won't – or you can't – speak, yet I like to think you might be able to understand me,' he murmured. 'If you can, then I need you to know how much I feel for the sacrifice you must have made. That I pray perhaps, one day, one of our kind may be able to make a similar gesture.'

He reached out, gently touching the side of the visitor's face with his fingertips. Surprisingly, it did not flinch away, as Terrell had half expected. Instead, it raised its own hand, covering his for the briefest possible moment.

A lump rose in Terrell's throat. 'You *do* understand, don't you?' he whispered, hardly daring to believe it himself.

If he had expected confirmation, he was disappointed. The visitor dropped its hand again, weakly stretching it out towards the writing desk.

It was as if it was reaching for something, Terrell told himself. He snatched up a pencil and a sheet of paper, thrusting them into the visitor's grasp. Trembling with anticipation, he watched and waited as the creature began to make marks upon the paper in a slow, laborious scrawl. Finally, eagerly, he took the paper back and studied it.

It was just a shape, perhaps a symbol of some kind. In human terms, Terrell thought it looked a bit like two teardrops laid on their sides, slightly overlapping. And beneath it, a line of smaller marks which suggested a form of writing.

So little, and so meaningless – yet it represented the first cultural exchange between two beings whose worlds were light years apart. It was with an overriding sense of awe that Terrell took the paper, folded it carefully and tucked it in his tunic pocket.

He mouthed his final goodbyes and left, feeling the same sense of loss he had known on the night his father died. He paused in the doorway and looked back, perhaps expecting just one word of farewell, but it was not to be. The visitor had laid down on the bunk again and was staring wretchedly up at the room's single window.

Louise was waiting for him in the corridor outside. She walked with him to the front door and out on to the drive, where they stopped.

'Will you write?' she asked.

Terrell forced a half-smile. 'If I can.' He glanced back towards the sanatorium. 'Look after him for me, won't you?'

She nodded. 'And you look after yourself.' She almost added 'for me' too, but thought it might sound too forward. 'Perhaps when you get leave . . .' she prompted, leaving the sentence unfinished.

Terrell hunched his shoulders slightly. 'We'll see.' He held out his hand, stiffly and awkwardly.

To shake it would have been too cold, too painful. Instead, Louise put on a brave smile and looked up into his eyes. 'That means goodbye, Charles. I won't say goodbye to you.'

She turned away before he could see the tears

welling up in her eyes and began walking back towards the sanatorium. Terrell watched her go, his own eyes slightly moist, wishing he could call after her but knowing he would not. A feeling of self-loathing rose in his chest, moving up to that dark, secret place in his mind which had blighted his life ever since he could remember. For perhaps the millionth time, he cursed that part of himself which was always detached, always on the outside. His *difference*.

Terrell was exhausted. He paused in his back-breaking work, leaning on the handle of his spade and sucking in deep, rejuvenating lung-fulls of the crisp night air. Finally rested, he straightened up and reviewed his efforts in the dim light of the jeep's shuttered headlights. The trench was almost completed; six more feet of soil to shift and he would join up with where he had started five hours previously.

He reached into his tunic pocket and pulled out the precious slip of paper yet again, checking the alien symbol against the giant pattern he had carved. From ground level, it was almost impossible to gauge the accuracy of his excavations. No draughtsman, Terrell could only hope that the finished pattern would present a fair representation when seen from above.

If, indeed, it *was* seen, and if there was anyone up there to see it, he reflected. Not for the first time, he questioned the sanity of his mission, even the soundness of his own mind. There were so many improbable things he had just taken for granted, accepted as fact without a shred of evidence to back them up.

Only one thought continued to make sense to him, glowing like a beacon light in a murky fog of uncertainty. The visitor and his companion had come to Earth for a purpose – and that purpose was of vital significance to the human race. Everything else about Terrell's plan was based on a single assumption: that they had not come alone.

Picking up the spade again, Terrell returned to his labour, knowing that he no longer had much choice anyway. He would not, could not, go back to war. His contact with the visitor had not so much changed him as complete a process which had already been started without his fully realising it.

Now he had passed the point of no return. He had already been AWOL for three days, and the stolen jeep and cans of precious, rationed gasoline merely compounded his crime. He wondered, idly, whether the British Army could still afford to shoot deserting officers. Or, if his mission was doomed to failure, whether he might be able to register as a conscientious objector.

With a grunt, Terrell dug out the last spadeful of earth and tossed it aside. Throwing down the spade, he walked over to the jeep and began unloading the cans of fuel, carrying them back to his excavations. He began to walk around the perimeter of the pattern, pouring the fuel into the shallow channel. Finally, when the last jerry-can was empty, he stood back, struck a match and tossed it into the trench.

Twin ribbons of blue flame licked out on either side, uncoiling outwards and around the con-toured depression like a pair of fiery serpents, finally devouring each other. The beacon flared in the dark. Two teardrops, laid on their sides and slightly overlapping.

There was nothing left to do but to wait. Terrell sank down on his haunches upon the damp ground, finally overcome with exhaustion. He looked upwards, straining his eyes into the black-ness of the night sky and wondering what was up there. It would be ironic, he thought, if he attracted nothing more than a stray German bomber.

Perhaps that would turn out to be his single, and final, contribution to the war effort – tricking the Luftwaffe into wasting their bombload on a deserted Hampshire field. He pricked his ears for the drone of engines, but it never came.

Feeling a shiver that racked his entire body, Terrell snapped back into full consciousness with a start, realising that he had been sleeping. The fiery symbol was almost out now, with just a few isolated patches of flame spluttering into extinc-tion. He shivered again, suddenly and uncontrol-lably – but it was not the coldness or the dampness of the night which had penetrated deep into his bones.

The sense of failure, that it had all been a ridiculous waste of effort, was overpowering. Regaining his full senses, Terrell dropped his head into his cupped hands and began to weep shamelessly.

To say that Terrell heard the sound of the approaching craft was a contradiction in terms, for it was completely noiseless. Indeed, it was the greater silence against the still of the night which first alerted him to the fact that something unusual was happening. That, and the subtle change in air pressure which suddenly enveloped his body, as though he had been wrapped up and cocooned in an invisible bubble. Then there was a blinding, bluish-white light, which seemed to have no apparent source. It just *was*, a circular pool of radiance which extended no more than two or three feet outwards around him and above his head.

There was a new warmth in the air, too – along with a sense of utter comfort, absolute peace.

Then Terrell sensed himself being lifted, or rather floated, off the ground. He felt weightless, free, exalted. He began to rise, up into the air, up towards the apparently dark and empty sky.

Up towards whatever it was that had come for him.

CHAPTER ONE

The deafening roar of the two Tornado F3s
shattered the night as they took off from 313
Fighter Squadron's base near the east coast of
Scotland. Sixty million pounds worth of world-
class defence engineering lifted off the tarmac
and tore up through the moonlit sky, out towards
the open sea. Scimitar One and Scimitar Two
were on a mission.

'Really, though, do you think I'm getting fat?'

An impish smile lifted the corners of Flight
Lieutenant Chris Drake's mouth as he looked out
of the cockpit at the clouds below. 'I wouldn't
worry about it. Some women like that,' he said to
his navigator. He could never resist teasing him.
Gerry was so good-natured that he was a joy to
wind up.

Flight Lieutenant Gerry Llewellyn's face
dropped. 'So I *am* getting fat, then?'

'I shouldn't think so. Your uniform's probably
shrinking, that's all.'

'You miserable . . . !'

Drake laughed. 'Look, this is a classic example

of transference. You're a slob who's never cared about your weight before. You're worried about Ange getting fat after the baby's born.'

'Thank you, Professor Freud, you complimentary swine.'

Suddenly, a message broke in over the radio.

'Scimitar Two, Scimitar Two, this is Scimitar One. Radar have re-established the fast-moving contact coming from the north-east. We are to make a high-altitude intercept.'

'Roger, Scimitar One.' Drake grinned again. 'Ready for some action, Gerry? Maybe we can get ourselves a war.'

Llewellyn's reply was cut short by another call over the radio.

'Intercept and identify only, Scimitar Two.'

'Roger, boss.'

Squadron Leader Haynes in Scimitar One didn't believe a word. *'Repeat, intercept and identify only. Am I clear, Scimitar Two?'*

'Roger, Scimitar One. Absolutely,' said Drake, innocently.

Gerry Llewellyn sighed. He didn't believe a word of it, either.

'Scimitar Two, this is Radar. What is your position?'

Llewellyn checked his co-ordinates. 'This is Scimitar Two, Scimitar Two, currently two hundred and fifty nautical miles north-east of Aberdeen.'

'Roger, Scimitar Two.'

Llewellyn looked out at the night sky. The

contact didn't seem to be within sight.

'Can you see anything yet?' he asked.

Drake scanned the horizon. 'Nope. Nothing on radar. Not visual.'

'So . . . what next with you and Sarah?' asked Llewellyn.

'The usual, I expect,' said Drake. 'You know.'

Llewellyn rolled his eyes. 'Chris, why can't you ever make the effort with a relationship and get yourself a steady girlfriend?'

'What do I need a girlfriend for when I've got you?'

Llewellyn laughed. It was almost true, in a way: the two of them worked together so much that sometimes it felt like he spent more time with Drake than he did with his wife.

'*Radar to Scimitar Two. Contact bearing zero-four-zero, range twenty-five miles. Are you visual?*'

Drake searched the sky. The contact should just about be visible by now. 'Not visual.'

'*Radar to Scimitar Two. Range fifteen miles.*'

Strange, thought Drake. 'This is Scimitar Two. Still not visual.'

'*Radar to Scimitar One. Are you visual?*'

'*Negative. Out of range.*'

Drake lifted an eyebrow. 'Quel surprise.'

'*Radar to Scimitar Two. Range ten miles. Are you visual?*'

'Not visual!' Drake couldn't understand it. Where was the contact?

'*Scimitar Two. Radar contact closing rapidly. What is visibility?*'

'We can see clear to Sweden,' said Drake, puzzled.

'It's Norway, actually,' interjected Llewellyn, irrelevantly.

'Radar to Scimitar Two. Contact separation negligible. Are you visual?'

Drake was about to reply when he saw it. It was like – well, he didn't know what it was like. Roundish, black but somehow emitting light, and moving faster and more smoothly than anything he'd ever seen before – it was certainly like no other aircraft in the world.

'Visual! Visual!'

Then it was gone.

'Scimitar Two, this is Radar. We have lost contact. What is your condition?'

Drake was shaken but untouched. 'Crew and aircraft undamaged, repeat undamaged. We have lost contact.'

'Scimitar Two, this is Scimitar One. Did you identify the aircraft?'

'Whatever that was, it was no aircraft!' blurted Drake.

'Scimitar Two, say again?'

'Disregard,' he said, frustratedly. 'Unable to identify. Radar have lost it.' And whatever it was, he'd let it get away.

Then Llewellyn saw it – sitting right on their tail. 'Six o'clock!' he shouted.

'Contact reacquired!' cried Drake. The adrenalin surged through his system. 'Hold on to your handbag, fat boy. It's not going to put one past us again.' He pulled on the flight column and the jet made a max rate turn, banking sharply to the right.

'We're not shaking it. Contact on our six o'clock – range half a mile!' Llewellyn tried to keep the stress out of his voice as the contact continued to tail them.

Drake's blood was rising. Whoever was flying that thing was keeping up their aggressive tailing despite every trick and manouevre he attempted. The Tornado F3 was outclassed and absolutely vulnerable at that range and position. Whatever it was was making a damned good job of intimidating them, and Scimitar One was nowhere in sight.

'Still on our six o'clock,' repeated Llewellyn.

'This is Scimitar Two. Contact on our six o'clock. Range half a mile. Holding formation, minimum separation. Taking evasive action,' called Drake.

'Scimitar Two, this is Scimitar One. You do not have clearance to treat the contact as hostile. Hang fire. Scimitar One closing to join you—'

Then silence as the systems went dead.

'Interference!' cried Drake. 'It must be some kind of weapon. Systems down, systems down.' What the hell kind of missile could knock out the entire flight systems of a plane like that?

Just as suddenly, the systems reactivated and they heard Squadron Leader Haynes come over the radio.

'Radar, Radar, this is Scimitar One. Temporary

loss of avionics, all systems now back on line. Not visual with Scimitar Two.'

'Radar, Radar, this is Scimitar Two. Contact broken off.' Drake was furious. 'Whatever it was, and whatever it did to us, we've lost it again.'

'Radar to Scimitar Two, we have a signal heading up through twenty thousand feet, bearing two-ninety.'

'Scimitar Two in pursuit. I'm going after him.'

Llewellyn was horrified. 'Chris, no – that thing's got to be doing at least mach 2 – all we're going to catch is its vortex!'

'Scimitar Two, contact has now passed above twenty-three thousand.'

This was madness. The F3 wasn't built to sustain these heights.

'Scimitar Two, this is Scimitar One. Abort intercept, abort intercept!'

Llewellyn was desperate. 'Chris, you're pushing the aircraft too hard!'

'He hit us with something – I'm going to hit him!'

'Scimitar Two, this is Scimitar One. Break off! You are ordered to break off!'

Drake was oblivious to the danger. He couldn't hear anything but the rush of blood through his head as he pushed the Tornado further and further beyond its limits.

'He's back!' cried Llewellyn as the contact came into view again.

'Scimitar Two engaging contact.' Drake's mind was totally focused, eyes fixed on the craft ahead, ready to fire – waiting, waiting for the perfect target . . .

'*Do not engage! Do not engage!*'

'Chris, break off!'

'*You are vetoed to engage!*'

Flight Lieutenant Drake held his breath and shot for home. The explosion was staggering.

Drake and Llewellyn vaguely heard the words 'unauthorised kill' come over the radio as the Tornado started to spin like a child's toy. It dropped like a stone through the sky.

'We're out of control!' Drake bellowed at the radio as he fought to subdue the jet.

'Fifteen thousand feet!' bawled Llewellyn.

Drake was pulling frantically on the flight column. 'I can't hold her!'

Llewellyn's heart was pounding and his stomach felt like it was trying to burst out of the roof of his mouth as he watched the altimeter spin down like something out of a disaster movie. 'Twelve thousand feet!'

'I can't get us out of this!' panicked Drake, grappling with the controls.

'Eight thousand feet – we're going in, eject, eject, eject!' roared Llewellyn.

'If you want to go, then go!' Drake couldn't believe this was happening to him. Surely there was *something* he could do?

'Three thousand feet!' barked Llewellyn. 'Chris – mayday, mayday, mayday, Scimitar Two, Tornado F3, 2 people on board, two hundred and fifty nautical miles north-east of Aberdeen. Navigator now ejecting aircraft.'

Llewellyn's hand reached for the ejector and pulled. Drake was alone in the plummeting craft.

'Radar to Scimitar Two, eject, eject, eject!'

Drake closed his eyes as he reached for the handle and pulled.

Nick Shay was doing what he always did when he was bored. He ate. The floor beneath his feet, littered with discarded candy bar wrappers, empty crisp packets and take-away food cartons, bore testimony to the tedium of his job.

The search for intelligent signals from space was a long, slow and so far totally unrewarding business – one of the main reasons that the Government had slashed their funding and turned the tracking station over to the M.o.D. Now there was only the boring routine work of monitoring satellite transmissions, with just Shay and Dr Tucker to man the facility on a part-time, shift-work basis.

But the *real* work, the original work, still went on, strictly unofficially and in volunteered, unpaid time. Dr Tucker had seen to that, using every trick in the book to keep it undercover.

Shay finished his chocolate bar and lolled back in his swivel chair, propping his feet up on the computer console in front of him and staring morosely at the row of blank screens. The printers, as ever, were silent. Tonight, yet again, ET wasn't making any phone calls – especially to SETI monitoring stations on Earth.

Shay sighed deeply, digging deep into his jacket pocket and finding a half-eaten bag of cheeselets. Extricating it, he began to investigate its contents.

There was a short bleeping sound, which indicated an incoming signal. One of the screens displayed a brief pulse line, which peaked at around six gigahertz and failed to evoke Shay's interest. It was nothing unusual – one or other of the orbital tracking satellites was always picking up a snatch of a stray signal rarely worth bothering with. Seconds later, the pulse flared again, this time higher up the band and with a more sustained signal. Almost simultaneously, one of the printers clacked into life and began to spew out massive amounts of data. This was extremely unusual. Suddenly, Shay was very interested indeed.

The packet of cheeselets flew out of his hands as he jumped upright in his chair. He kicked out at the console, propelling himself across to the gushing printer. Feeding the readout through his fingers, he scanned the figures with a quick and practised eye. Just a cursory glance was enough to tell him this was something out of the ordinary. Whistling through his teeth, he reached for the phone.

Amanda Tucker's mobile purred into life. Propped up against the pillows, her daughter

Emily pouted. 'I suppose that means no bedtime story tonight,' she complained.

Amanda smiled. 'We'll see. It's probably nothing important.' She brought the phone up to her ear. 'This had better be good. You just spoiled a ten-year-old's bedtime.'

'Amanda, it's me, Nick. Listen, one of the satellites just picked up something really weird. Pulses in a very narrow bandwidth at 8.6 gigahertz. Highly refined beam. And it's outgoing, not incoming.'

Amanda's smile faded. 'Are you sure?'

'Like I said – weird, huh? Look, I know you're not supposed to be on call tonight, but . . .' He never got a chance to finish the sentence.

'For something like this, I'm on call *every* night,' Amanda cut in. 'I'll be there in fifteen minutes.' She snapped off the phone, her blue eyes sparkling.

Emily pulled a face at her mother. 'Now I *know* I'm not going to get a story.'

Amanda pulled back the bedclothes. 'Even better – you get to stay up late,' she promised. 'We've got to go to the tracking station.'

Emily perked up at once, her bedtime story forgotten. A visit to the station invariably carried fringe benefits. Nick usually had a seemingly endless supply of chocolate bars.

Amanda replayed the recording of the signal transmission on the monitor for the third time whilst riffling through the accompanying pages of print-out data, struggling to make sense of any of it.

'Told you it was weird, didn't I?' Shay said, looking over her shoulder. 'Worth a late-night call?'

Amanda nodded. 'You bet. And you think we just happened to pick it up by accident?'

Shay hunched his shoulders. 'You tell me. It was on such a narrow beam that it's a chance in a million our satellite would be in the right place at the right time.'

'So no one else will have this right now?'

Shay attempted to suppress a smile of triumph, and failed. 'Nope. Just us. What you might call a world exclusive.'

Amanda sucked at her teeth. 'So where has it come from?'

Shay checked his own preliminary figures. 'Best guess, somewhere above the northern British Isles, very high altitude.'

'But if the satellite passed through the beam?' Amanda muttered, frowning.

'Exactly,' Shay said, with heavy emphasis. 'That signal was aimed *outwards* – out into space.'

Amanda considered this for a few seconds, finally shaking her head. 'But that doesn't make sense. We've got nothing up there in the path of this beam. No satellites, no probes . . . nothing.'

'Then it was intended for deep space,' Shay put in, drawing the obvious conclusion. 'Deep, deep space.'

Curled up on a day bed, Emily stirred. 'Who's in space?' she demanded drowsily.

'No one,' her mother hastened to assure her. 'No one at all.' Her eyes met Shay's in a sideways, meaningful glance. She dropped her voice to a whisper. 'At least no one we know of.'

Pacified, Emily turned over and went back to sleep. Amanda turned her full attention back to the recorded transmission. The closer she studied it, the more baffling it became.

'There's just nothing in here to get a hook on. Not one part of it is anything like a normal transmission. And the fact that it was aimed far out into space.'

'But it came from Earth,' Shay reminded her.

Amanda shook her head. 'No, it came from *near* Earth. High up in the sky. Someone was up there – someone or something.'

One of the computers bleeped. Its dedicated printer emitted a faint whirring sound, signalling an imminent print-out. 'Maybe they're still up there,' Shay muttered. 'I think it's starting up again.' Even as he spoke, the equipment burst into life again.

Watching the transmission live, as it were, for the first time, Amanda felt an overpowering sense of awe. It was as if Time itself had paused for an instant, just to sweep her up and carry her along in its flow. A blip in history, perhaps the most important and significant blip in mankind's entire existence.

Shay felt it too. His tone was almost reverential.

'What does it mean?' he murmured. 'What are they saying?'

They were unanswerable questions. 'More to the point,' Amanda added quietly, 'who's listening?'

The computer screen suddenly flared, as though someone had just turned up the brilliance control. The banded pattern of the transmission disappeared momentarily, then began to reform, oddly distorted. It began to break up into jagged, irregularly shaped lines. The printer's furious clacking intensified for a few more seconds, then ceased abruptly.

Shay's immediate reaction was one of panic. 'What the hell's happening? Is the equipment malfunctioning?'

Amanda steeled herself to calm objectivity. She hurried across to study the last few seconds of print-out. Everything seemed to be in perfect working order. It was just as if the transmission itself had been cut off in mid-flow. There was a long period of silence.

Finally, Shay spoke again, recovering his composure. 'What now?' he wanted to know.

Amanda nodded over at her daughter, who was by now sleeping soundly. 'I think Emily's got the right idea,' she said quietly. 'We should both try to get some rest.'

The sound of a car pulling up outside woke Amanda from a light and fitful doze, slumped across the computer console. She rose from her chair, crossing to the window. She recognised the grey Lexus immediately, and knew it meant trouble. Although he was technically in charge of the monitoring station, Edward Fleming only made one of his rare visits when it was something really important.

She hurried back to Shay, sleeping uncomfortably across a couple of chairs. She prodded him violently, hissing into his ear. 'Nick, we have a problem, Fleming's here.'

Shay shook himself awake. 'Trouble?'

Amanda's mouth was set in a firm, determined line. 'Not if I can help it.' She waved her hand over towards the computer read-outs. 'Hide all this stuff. I'll try to head him off.'

Composing herself, Amanda stepped outside into the corridor to intercept their unwelcome visitor.

'Edward, how nice to see you. To what do we owe this rare and honoured visit?' she asked pleasantly.

Fleming looked unimpressed. In his usual, brusque manner, he came straight to the point. 'Did we pick up a radio transmission last night?'

Amanda feigned surprise. Her blue eyes radiated innocence. 'What kind of a transmission?'

'Something out of the ordinary, perhaps?' Fleming said, guardedly. He wasn't sure how much he was supposed to reveal.

He was no match for Amanda. 'I'm not quite sure I follow you, Edward. What exactly do you mean, out of the ordinary?'

Fleming took the bait. He coughed, nervously.

'I've had a call from the Ministry of Defence,' he admitted. 'Apparently there was some un-usual . . . *activity* last night.'

'Perhaps if you could be more specific, I'd know what to look for,' Amanda suggested.

Fleming gave up the unequal struggle. 'A high-energy transmission. Something powerful enough to throw an aircraft's avionics and guid-ance systems completely off-line for several sec-onds. The M.o.D. seemed to think we might have picked it up.'

Amanda thought deeply for a moment, finally shaking her head. 'No, nothing like that I can think of,' she lied. 'So where did this transmission originate?'

Fleming shrugged. 'That's just it. No one seems able to figure it out. An RAF Tornado pilot on routine patrol reported sighting an unidentified aircraft some two hundred and fifty nautical miles north-east of Aberdeen. Moments later his instru-ments and those of the fighter control ground station were hit by this incredibly powerful trans-mission. The Tornado went down in the North Sea and they're searching for the pilot now.'

Amanda digested all this information, slotting it into place with her own observations. She fought desperately to conceal her excitement as a composite picture started to fall into place. There were just a few vital pieces missing.

'And the mystery aircraft? What happened to that?'

Fleming looked sheepish. 'They wouldn't tell

me much about that. Only that the Tornado pilot loosed off a missile before he went down. Ground control picked up a trace of some kind of escape pod being ejected, and the Army are searching for that, too.'

He fell silent. Amanda realised that he had told her as much as he knew himself. It was time to bring the visit to a conclusion as soon as possible. She walked Fleming down the corridor towards the exit.

'Well of course I'll search through last night's recordings to see what I can find,' she promised. 'I'll let you know immediately if I turn anything up.'

As soon as he was gone, Amanda raced back to the monitoring room. Shay was hunched over one of the computers, studying something he'd called up on the internet.

'Did you hear any of that?' Amanda asked him.

Shay nodded. 'Most of it.' He paused a moment. 'Look, we can't keep this all to ourselves forever.'

Amanda's eyes blazed. 'They took our work away from us, Nick. I'm not going to let them do it again. This could be what we've been looking for all this time.' She caught the look of doubt which crossed Shay's face. 'Look at it this way – we've analysed the composition of that transmission every way we know, right?'

Shay shrugged. 'And it still doesn't make sense. That doesn't tell us anything.'

'Suppose the reason we can't read it is because no one on Earth sent it?'

Shay looked at her in puzzlement. 'But we can be pretty sure that it only came from a few hundred miles away. It has to have come from a human source, surely?'

Amanda realised she wasn't getting her point across. She rephrased her earlier statement. 'Sorry – I didn't mean no one *on* Earth. I meant no one *from* Earth.'

Shay finally fell in. His eyes widened. 'You're talking about a non-human intelligence. Already here. Trying to make contact with others far out in space.'

Amanda nodded. 'Exactly. Perhaps to whoever sent them – and sent them for a reason.'

Shay was deeply reflective for several seconds. 'Know what I think? That radio burst Fleming was talking about – the one which knocked out the Tornado's avionics. That could be what interfered with our transmission as well.'

It took Amanda a few moments to work out the full implications of this theory. 'Are you suggesting that it might have come from a completely different source?'

Shay sucked at his teeth. 'It's a thought, isn't it? There's something else, too.' He jabbed his thumb at the computer screen. 'I just picked up this little item on one of the UFO web sites. Supposed crash landing in the wilds of Scotland.'

It was Amanda's turn to look dubious. 'So somebody else has never noticed the planet Venus before. We occasionally get meteorites. Where do all these cranks come from, anyway?'

Shay paused for dramatic effect. 'The timing of that reported sighting just happens to coincide almost exactly with the satellite transmission,' he pointed out.

Amanda's attitude changed abruptly. She thought deeply for a few seconds. 'I'm going to go up there,' she announced finally, impulsively.

Shay was doubtful. 'What do you expect to find out? No one's going to tell you anything.'

Amanda grinned. 'One of the few benefits of working for the Ministry of Defence is that you get a Grade One security clearance,' she pointed out. 'With any luck, I should be able to bluff my way through long enough to find out what I need to know.'

Shay glanced across to Emily, who was just beginning to wake up. 'What about Emily?'

Amanda smiled again. 'What are grandmothers for?' she asked.

CHAPTER TWO

Flight Lieutenant Chris Drake began to emerge from a sedative-induced sleep into a world of bland, uniform whiteness. Full consciousness returned slowly, and with it the problems of differentiating between what might have been nightmare and what had been reality.

Fully awake, the realisation that virtually nothing had been a dream came as a shock. The darkness, the stars, the cold, cold sea – it had been real. The crash had been real. The UFO had been real. *Now* was real. Drake took stock of his surroundings.

He was in a hospital bed, he realised. His ribs felt sore and he had a blinding headache. There was an RAF doctor standing over him. His face, deeply pockmarked, was stern but not unkindly.

'Good to see you're back with us, Flight Lieutenant,' the medic murmured. 'You're a lucky man. Another hour on that life-raft and you'd have died from exposure.'

Drake didn't feel lucky. It seemed like a full-scale dogfight was going on inside his head.

Suddenly he remembered Gerry, and his own problems didn't seem very important anymore.

'My navigator?' he enquired weakly.

Wing Commander Friday lowered his eyes slightly. 'Flight Lieutenant Llewellyn sustained a fractured femur and humerus on ejection. We believe these injuries were responsible for his inability to enter his life-raft. He was found in the water, having died from exposure. I'm very sorry,' he added, gently.

Drake gasped. He felt as if he'd been punched in the stomach. 'Gerry,' he whispered.

A wave of nausea came over him and he struggled to keep a grip as a hundred different memories he and Gerry had shared flew through his mind. The time Gerry had taken the blame when Drake smashed up a jeep trying to impress some girl; him and Gerry passing out of the academy together; spending Christmas with Gerry and his kind, gentle old parents; Gerry's wedding where Drake had been so proud to be his best man; Gerry asking him to be the long-awaited baby's godfather; Gerry urging him not to pursue the contact . . . and now Gerry was dead and he was still alive.

It suddenly occurred to him that Friday was still speaking.

'. . . I'm pleased to be able to tell you that your own injuries were minor, and should respond to conservative treatment.'

Another realisation brought another wave of nausea. 'Gerry's wife. How's she taking it?'

Friday paused. 'She's been admitted to our labour ward. The shock appears to have brought things on ahead of time.'

Drake put his head in his hands as Friday coughed apologetically. 'You have visitors who've been waiting to talk to you,' he said. 'Though I have put it on record that I don't think you're up to debriefing right now, but they were very insistent.'

As if on cue, he stepped back from Drake's bed and the two officers who had been hovering in the background approached.

Drake stared at them, still numb with grief and shock. From her uniform, the woman was obviously RAF, but the man with her was a surprise. He was in his mid-fifties and he radiated an aura of absolute authority. Tall, wide-shouldered, craggy. A big man in every sense of the word. His uniform identified him as a Major General in the United States Air Force, and Drake was immediately puzzled as to why the Americans should be involved.

Introductions were brief and businesslike.

'I'm Reece. NATO. This is Squadron Leader Knox. She's been assigned to me by the RAF. Sorry to hear about your navigator. I need you to describe what kind of aircraft you fired upon.'

'We've been played the RT record of your sortie,' said Knox. She looked briefly at her notes. 'Your words were: "Whatever that was, it was no aircraft." '

Drake was still trying to figure out why the

Americans should be interested.

'With respect, General – but I don't understand what any of this has to do with you, sir?'

Knox flashed him an admonishing glance, but Reece appeared prepared to explain. 'I'm the commander tasked by NATO to respond to breaches of European airspace by non-NATO aircraft. I work in concert with the military of the country or countries involved – in this case, your Royal Air Force. Now please describe the aircraft.'

The man wanted it straight, Drake thought. Here goes. 'Sir, what I saw was not an aircraft of any known type or design. I observed a luminous object, approximately twice our size, roughly spherical and with no apparent aerofoil surfaces.'

'Any identifying markings? Which country was it from?' Knox put in.

Drake regarded her with faint disbelief. 'Don't you get it? Didn't you hear what I said, ma'am? It was no aircraft.'

'Why did you engage it?' Reece demanded. 'Your orders were to observe and report.'

'Sir, we were hit with some sort of electronic weapon which knocked out all instrumentation. I believed we were under attack. I couldn't let it get away.' Drake scanned the two officers' faces for a glimmer of understanding but saw only open scepticism. He felt the need to justify himself. 'Look, we were alone up there. You can't even begin to understand if you didn't see that thing. I made a judgement call – and it was the right one.'

Reece frowned. 'You fired without authorisation. You directly disobeyed your orders. You've created one hell of a mess for us to deal with. Basically, you're in deep trouble, Flight Lieutenant Drake.'

That was probably an understatement, Drake thought miserably. Gerry was dead and there was no one to back up his story. Unbidden, those last few seconds in the Tornado flashed into his mind. Perhaps there *was* a way of verifying his story.

'Look, maybe that thing ejected some kind of escape pod,' he said. 'Ground Control might have picked it up on radar. Find that and it'll prove that what I'm telling you is the truth.'

Knox and the General exchanged a telling glance.

'Ground Control *did* track something,' Reece conceded eventually. 'Your military are still out searching for any kind of wreckage.'

Drake felt a glimpse of relief in his world of darkness. There was still a chance that he would be vindicated. This temporary boost to his spirits was immediately cancelled out by Squadron Leader Knox's next words, however.

'In the meantime, you're grounded, Flight Lieutenant Drake – pending the results of an official enquiry. The doctor says you should be fit enough to be discharged in a day or so. As of then, consider yourself on leave until further notice.'

'It's easy for you, isn't it, sitting about down here, giving me a slap on the wrists and telling me I'm in deep trouble,' said Drake, bitterly. 'If it had been you up there, if you'd seen that thing, you'd realise we could *all* soon be in deep trouble.'

A few hours later, Drake was wide awake again. Exhausted by the interview and his injuries, he'd fallen into a troubled, fitful sleep, peppered with nightmares. Moving was agony, but he couldn't stay in bed any longer without facing Gerry's wife – no, God help her, his *widow*, Ange.

Drake manoeuvred himself clumsily out of bed and limped down the corridor, leaning on a walking stick like a frail old man. The five-minute walk to the maternity ward was the longest walk of his life. Finally, with his heart in his mouth, he opened the door to the unit and made his way over to Angela Llewellyn. It took all the courage he had to hobble over to her bed.

She was sitting up, staring at him as if he was a ghost. Drake could see her baby lying next to her, asleep in its cot, blissfully unaware of the tragedy into which it had been born.

'Hello, Ange,' croaked Drake, awkwardly. 'How are you?'

She was silent, still staring at him.

'I never thought . . . I'm so sorry, Ange.'

'They won't tell me what happened,' said Ange, tonelessly. 'Classified.'

'If I knew, I'd tell you. Believe me, I still don't.'

Ange got out of bed as her baby started to cry.

She smiled sadly, picking it up and cradling it to her. 'He'd been so good tonight,' she whispered, kissing its downy new-born head. She was silent for a while as she comforted her child.

Then she spoke again, without even looking at Drake. 'They say if you'd ejected with Gerry like you were supposed to, you'd have landed close enough to help him. I hope one day my son will be able to forgive you for taking his father away. I never will.'

Drake backed out of the room, blinded by the tears.

A swathe of fir trees decapitated at descending, stepped levels marked out the oblique trajectory of the crashing escape pod. Deflected and cushioned by these successive impacts, the craft had managed to clear the main body of the woods to land in open ground, carving a deep furrow in the marshy heathland before it finally came to rest.

Even covered in mud and half-buried, it looked utterly alien to the earth in which it was embedded. Yet its pilot, despite his spacesuit, lay coiled, foetus-like upon the ground as though he had returned home to the womb which had borne him.

Miraculously, he was not dead. The comparatively soft landing had saved the pod from total destruction, although the final impact had been enough to trigger off the escape hatch mechanism. Thrown clear of the crash site, he lay some ten feet from the main body of wreckage, his pressurised spacesuit still connected to the pod's life support system by a thin, metallic and flexible umbilical cord. It was this which had kept him alive through the long night as he drifted in and out of consciousness.

Full consciousness finally returned, and with it the cold dread of realisation. A cold shiver rippled through his frail body. If the pod's automatic homing beacon had been transmitting all that time . . .

Fear gave him strength. The pilot heaved himself into a sitting position, disconnecting the umbilical. He struggled to stand upright, only to collapse weakly again as the full force of Earth's gravity sucked at his body, draining every ounce of energy from his muscles. It had been so long. There was so much he had forgotten. He waited for a few seconds for his pumping heart to slow down and tried again, this time more cautiously. Slowly, feeling as though he had a sack of bricks on his back, he hauled himself first on to his knees and then to his feet. He looked around, surveying the bleak Scottish terrain. Apart from the isolated copse into which he had nearly crashed, there was nothing else to break up the barren landscape. It was open heathland on all sides, for as far as the eye could see. To seek cover, he would have to move on. With every step a major effort, he began to stumble away from the wreck.

The clatter of a helicopter in the sky above made him stop temporarily in his tracks to glance upwards. It was circling slowly at around eight hundred feet, perhaps half a mile or so behind him. As he watched, the craft completed its sweep and flew away eastwards.

He took only minor comfort from watching it depart. It was only a momentary respite from the lesser of the twin dangers which confronted him. In this exposed heathland it could only be a matter of time before they spotted him. The helicopter would give him some warning that his human predators, at least, were closing in. The *others*, if and when they came for him, would not give such clear warning.

He found himself almost wishing that the helicopter would turn back, and make another sweep right now. Capture and interrogation would probably be infinitely more humane than his secondary fate. Then he remembered the importance of his mission, the sense of purpose which had driven him across light-years of space to this tiny, almost achingly beautiful little blue-green planet. He could not afford to let himself be taken. Not yet. Not while there was still some hope.

He reached down to the waistband of his space-suit, unclipping his portable field computer and checking it out. It appeared to be undamaged. He switched it on, set it to transmit a tightly banded and coded signal and clipped it back into position. There was always the third possibility of rescue. Taking slight comfort from this thought, he steeled himself to struggle onwards once again, with no clear destination in sight or mind. Somewhere to hole up, perhaps, to take cover and pray for that slim third alternative.

Flight Lieutenant Radcliffe led his men through the trees, emerging into the open again in clear view of the crashed pod. He froze, completely mesmerised by its weird, alien appearance.

Behind him, Sergeant Tuffley slipped the safety catch off his rifle with a meaningful click. 'Do we assume it's hostile, sir?' he wanted to know.

Radcliffe snapped back to the job in hand. 'Any survivors to be taken alive,' he hissed. 'Now have the rest of the men fan out and surround that thing. We go in slow – and very, very cautiously.'

The pilot reached a small clump of gorse bushes. In his utter exhaustion, they looked as inviting as a fully camouflaged dug-out. He sank down behind the largest bush gratefully, fighting to regain his breath. Finally, he unclipped his survival pack and unloaded it upon the ground. Even shedding this meagre weight brought a measure of relief. He suddenly realised how hungry he was. Opening the pack, he pulled out a clear envelope containing a vaguely greenish gel. Tearing it open, he put it to his mouth and gulped down the contents.

Nutrition taken care of, he turned his attention to his field computer, still dutifully transmitting its distress signal. There was no indication that the signal was being heard, let alone being responded to. Impatiently, he punched out a new digital sequence, switching to a different band. A small green light winked momentarily, followed by a faint bleeping sound.

The pilot's spirits soared. He dared to hope. Perhaps that third possibility was still open to him, even now. He repeated the call signal, confirming his position.

The screen came to life. A star map, distant and alien. As the pilot watched it intently, the image dissolved into a representation of the solar system, zeroing in on the third planet. Earth sprang into view, blue and white and brown – and beautiful. A small cursor traversed the continents, locating the British Isles and moving northwards. The computer began to bleep out a continuous, high-pitched note as it tracked in the returning transmission.

The tone changed, abruptly and menacingly. No longer merely tracking the signal, the computer had identified its source – and the tone was now harsher, more alarm-like.

The pilot felt a cold sickness spreading through his body as his worst fears were confirmed. *They* were already here. Perhaps they always had been. He threw the computer to the ground, stamping on it, smashing it to pieces. Forcing himself to his feet, he stumbled away in blind terror, abandoning everything. He did not look back.

Behind him, the air appeared to be shimmering, like the mirages above a country road on a hot day. The stunted gorse bushes seemed to tremble, their shapes weirdly distorted. There was a fizzing, crackling sound of raw energy, accompanied by a sudden burst of impossibly bright light.

Against it, the materialising figure appeared only as a dark shadow – huge, shapeless and unidentifiable. But malevolent, definitely malevolent. The image moved, appearing to change its shape and dimensions as it did so. Then, almost as quickly as it had manifested itself, it began to flicker and fade again. The crackling sounds died away. The light dulled, until it was just the orange glow of the gorse bushes, their dry foliage blazing with flames like some modern-day version of the biblical legend.

Satisfied that the pod was empty, Radcliffe gathered his men together to await further orders. Tuffley was on the field telephone, speaking to the helicopter pilot.

'They've spotted him, sir,' he called to Radcliffe. 'About a mile and a half from our present position. Do I call the chopper down for an airlift?'

Radcliffe nodded assent. He called the men into line as the helicopter swooped in for a landing.

The pilot had come to a small gorge, carved over the years by the small but fast-flowing stream which drained the heathland. On the other side, the flat land gave way to a ridge of hills, surmounted by dense woodland. Once in the trees, he could find cover, he would be comparatively safe. There was only the problem of getting up there.

A steep, near-vertical wall of loose shale seemed the most direct route. The pilot splashed his way across the stream, taking things slowly, conserving his energy for the climb ahead.

His wet boots helped give him purchase on the dry, slippery surface. Laboriously, every step a herculean effort, he started to scramble up the slope.

The clatter of the returning helicopter made him pause, laying flat and belly-down to stop him from sliding back down. The sound of the helicopter's engines was different now – somehow more purposeful, and growing steadily louder by the second. The pilot had no doubts that it was no longer merely sweeping hopefully. They had located his position now, and were closing in fast.

He redoubled his efforts to reach the top of the wall, his lungs almost at bursting point.

The chopper dropped on to firm ground some hundred yards from the stream. The men poured out, fanning into an attack position. Radcliffe fingered the field binoculars around his neck, then decided he didn't really need them. He had a clear enough view of his quarry. Against the light grey of the shale, the dark material of his flightsuit made him stand out like an inkblot on virgin paper. He was about half-way up the slope, gaining height rapidly.

Tuffley gestured up to the trees on the top of the hill. 'If he gets up there, sir, we've lost him,' he pointed out, voicing the obvious. 'He could hide out in those trees for days.' He unslung his rifle from his shoulder, cocking it. 'Shall I bring him down, sir?'

Without waiting for an answer, Tuffley dropped to his knees, assumed a firing position and took aim. Radcliffe's hand dropped to his shoulder. 'No, wait.'

No matter where he came from, who he was working for, the pilot was a fellow airman, doing his job. He deserved a chance, Radcliffe thought. He raised his hands to his mouth, cupping them into a makeshift megaphone.

'Stop where you are! Don't try to escape. We don't want to have to open fire.'

The pilot gave no sign that he had heard, although Radcliffe knew that it was impossible that he had not. He kept on climbing, now nearly three-quarters of the way up the face.

'Stop, or we'll shoot!'

'Sir, we can't let him get away,' Tuffley said urgently.

Radcliffe knew it. He shouted again. 'Stop! Stop now.'

The pilot was still climbing, nearing the top. They were running out of time.

'Fire,' Radcliffe muttered, reluctantly.

Tuffley fired a single shot. The climbing figure jerked, and was still, starting to slide back down the shale. He hit a small outcrop of more solid rock and stopped. A few moments passed, and he moved again. He wasn't dead.

The pilot's hand moved up to a small control panel on the shoulder of his flightsuit and pressed a recessed button. Radcliffe and Tuffley stared in disbelief as the area immediately around his body seemed to shimmer. The pilot's suited form appeared to flicker off and on a couple of times then fade to a ghost image like on a faulty TV set. Finally, he melted completely into invisibility, merging with his background.

Tuffley gaped up at his superior, his eyes wide and disbelieving. 'Christ Almighty. How'd he do that?' he wanted to know.

Radcliffe didn't even attempt an answer. His eyes were still fixed firmly on the spot where the pilot had disappeared. As he watched, a few loose pieces of shale started to slide back down the face, quickly growing into a minor avalanche. Something, something big, was falling back down the slope towards the stream. And then there was nothing.

The pilot somehow kept running, punch-drunk and in agony, knowing that his last attempt at evading capture had been no more than a token gesture. When he had destroyed his field computer, he had also destroyed his power-pack. Without it, the suit's active camouflage emitter was good for three, four minutes at the most. He had to get to the woods before he became visible again, or the soldiers would find him anyway.

Somehow, he made it. Somehow, stumbling through the undergrowth, his face contorted with pain, he came to the shelter of the trees at last. Now fighting desperately to retain consciousness, the pilot lurched from tree to tree before finally losing his balance and pitching over a high bank. It seemed like he tumbled for ages before coming to land on a solid, hard surface.

Charles Terrell's last thoughts before falling into coma were that he had achieved nothing. And he wondered, bitterly, briefly, if it had all been worth it.

CHAPTER THREE

The Scottish police were so nice, Amanda Tucker reflected, with the easy magnanimity of someone who has got what they wanted. As soon as he'd seen her ID, Inspector Boyd of Kirkhaven police station couldn't have been more helpful.

'Though why the M.o.D. needed to send someone out about alleged UFO sightings, I can't imagine,' he'd said. 'Some of these people haven't even seen anything. They've just heard that the RAF have been out here, looking for the wreckage of an aircraft they lost. It's odd, because the only base around here's about forty miles away and it's been disused for a long while.'

Approaching the old RAF station along a neglected and overgrown track, Amanda could see from the rusted wire perimeter fences and weed-festooned tarmac that it had obviously been abandoned for years. Today, however, it was a hive of frenzied activity. Trucks were speeding along the concrete roads, helicopters were lined up in one area and she could see plenty of small green figures rushing about in the distance.

A thin smile of satisfaction crossed Amanda's lips. If there was a bit of a panic on, so much the better. It might make her task of bluffing her way in a little easier. Looking a lot more confident than she actually felt, she drove up to the gate, winding down her window.

The sentry regarded her dourly. 'Sorry, ma'am. This area is off-limits to civilian personnel.'

Amanda smiled. 'I know. That's why I'm here.' She flashed her M.o.D. security pass. 'So let's not mess about, eh? I've had to come a long way.'

Another car drew up behind her, honking its horn in its rush to get in. It had the desired effect. The sentry stepped back, waving her through. 'Check in with the guard room, ma'am.'

'Thanks.' Amanda smiled at him again and drove through the gates. Her luck held as she reached the guard room, as all the personnel were busy checking the contents of a military lorry. Unchallenged, she drove straight on past towards one of the aircraft hangars which appeared to be the main focus of attention. No one seemed to be paying her any attention. With an increasing feeling of confidence, Amanda parked next to a line of trucks and got out. Trying to look as casual as possible, she walked towards the hangar.

It appeared to be a good time. A little cluster of military personnel had started to gather outside the hangar's closed doors, as though they were expecting something to happen. Noting an

American uniform among them, Amanda wondered what a USAF Major General was doing on an RAF airbase.

Major General Reece and Squadron Leader Knox waited impatiently as the hangar doors began to open. They stepped through, catching their first glimpse of the crashed escape pod just as daylight began to flood into the hangar's gloomy interior. The gleaming metal of the pod seemed to materialise out of the dark. It was an awesome sight.

Reece caught his breath. 'My God. Maybe Drake was right.'

Sceptical as ever, Knox sniffed. 'With respect, sir – you're not falling for that crazy story of his, are you? We'll soon have the answer to which country's behind this.'

Reece continued to stare at the alien craft, transfixed. 'Helen – just *look* at it, for chrissakes. You seriously believe one of our military rivals produced that?'

Knox looked chagrined. 'We've just been temporarily wrong-footed, that's all. Unprepared for someone to have made a breakthrough advance of this kind.'

Reece wasn't really listening. His attention was concentrated on the pod.

'No country's ever prepared for its next war,' he murmured. 'Only for its last.' After a while, he seemed to come to a decision. 'Hold off on our report.'

'Sir?' Knox failed to understand.

'We can't just give them what we have. It won't be enough. I need proof, so they'll listen.'

Knox was about to argue, but thought better of it. Reece seemed to have made up his mind. She fell into step behind him as he took one last, incredulous look at the pod and strode off.

The hangar doors were already closing again as Amanda reached them. She got only a glimpse of its contents, but it was enough. Enough to tell her she had stumbled upon the biggest and most important discovery of her life. It was an awesome thought.

Amanda realised that she had to leave the base before it occurred to whomever she was supposed to report to that she'd breached security. She had to find out what this thing was, what it meant.

Feeling like a figment of someone else's dream, she made her way back to the car. She was out through the gates and driving back down the track before she suddenly realised she had absolutely no idea of where to go, or what to do next. She came to a crossroads, making an arbitrary choice to go back to the sleepy little town of Kirkhaven.

A few miles further down the road, her mobile phone purred. Amanda pulled in to the side of the road to answer it.

It was Nick Shay, and he sounded agitated.

'Look, Amanda, I think I've figured something

out. That radio burst which interrupted our transmission – it's from a completely different source and with a completely different signature.'

'You mean another transmission on the same wavelength?' Amanda asked.

'More than that. I'm pretty sure it was a deliberate attempt to jam the original. I think someone, somewhere, didn't want that message to get out, whatever it was.'

Amanda frowned. 'Somewhere?' she echoed. 'Where did the second transmission originate?'

There was a slight pause as Shay sighed. 'That's the bit I haven't worked out yet. It doesn't seem to come from anywhere – not from Earth, not from space. It just appears suddenly – almost as though it has just burst through into the upper atmosphere.'

Amanda was baffled, and she admitted it. 'I don't understand.'

Another, longer sigh. 'No, neither do I. But the fact remains that somebody wanted to block off that transmission. The question is, why?'

Amanda could tell from Shay's tone that it was a rhetorical question. 'But you have a theory?' she prompted.

'Suppose we're actually dealing with two different alien forces. Perhaps enemies of each other, even at war. Imagine that scenario and it starts to make some sense.'

It sounded preposterous, but after what she had seen in the hangar, Amanda wasn't prepared to dismiss anything lightly. 'I'll think about it,' she promised. 'In the meantime, keep trying to decipher what we've got.'

'Yeah, sure.' Shay paused. 'Just one other thing to keep in mind. If my theory is right, and these two forces are at war – they might not stop at just jamming each other's transmissions. So take it easy, do you hear me?'

Amanda nodded. 'I hear you.' She hung up and sat back to collect her thoughts into some kind of logical sequence. It wasn't easy. The events of the last half-hour swirled through her mind like wisps of fog, refusing to coagulate into any recognisable shape or form.

She'd seen proof with her own eyes of what she'd only guessed at, what she and Nick had been searching for traces of for years. She felt as if she'd been peeping in at Roswell.

Through the windscreen of the car, Amanda could see a small country pub a few hundred yards up the road. Suddenly, she decided that she needed a drink, and some time to switch off her overworking brain.

Chris Drake sat alone at a table cradling a generous measure of twelve-year-old single malt whisky with a dual purpose in mind: firstly to drown his sorrows and secondly to numb the continuing pain in his ribs. As well as the guilt and anguish of losing Gerry, he'd lived for flying for nearly fifteen years, and the shame of being grounded had shaken him to the core. Being confined to a hospital bed had made it seem like a prison sentence, so he'd discharged himself against medical advice.

He'd tried calling Sarah for some company, only to come to the humiliating realisation that she had been using him as much as he'd been using her before the crash. She was only interested in the successful pilot, not the grounded, limping, grieving man. She couldn't get off the phone fast enough. How often he'd said those same meaningless words, 'see you around', without ever realising how cruel they could sound.

The sight of a young, highly attractive blonde woman entering the otherwise empty pub was something of an antidote to the first, if not the second of his complaints. Drake visibly brightened. He watched Amanda as she approached the bar and bought half a lager. He had his favourite chat-up line ready for her as she turned towards him.

'This place gets pretty crowded, so I saved you a seat,' he announced, pushing a spare chair out with his foot.

Amanda hesitated, weighing him up in balance against all the usual arguments about talking to strange men in bars. It was a close call. He seemed affable enough, his line of patter was mildly amusing if not totally original, and there was no denying his physical attractiveness.

As if reading her thoughts, Drake spread his hands and hunched his shoulders in an extravagant shrug. The gesture could have said 'please yourself', or 'what harm can it do?' or simply 'I don't care'. Other than that it was neutral, harmless.

Amanda made up her mind. She walked over to Drake's table, accepting the proffered chair. Some casual, meaningless conversation might be exactly what she needed right now, she thought. 'Thanks for the tip. I'll take you up on it.'

She sat down, sipping at her drink and eyeing Drake over the rim of the glass. 'So, you're not from around here, are you?' she said, opening the conversation.

Drake shook his head. 'They tend to move us around from base to base. I'm in the RAF.' He detected a sudden glimmer of interest in Amanda's blue eyes and was surprised. She didn't look like the sort of woman who would be impressed by the old 'I'm a jet fighter pilot' routine. 'How could you tell?' he asked.

Amanda grinned. 'Both your eyes point in the same direction.' She extended her hand over the table. 'My name's Amanda, by the way.'

Drake smiled, shaking her hand, keeping it formal with just a hint of intimacy. 'I'm Chris. You're not local, either. So what brings you up to the wilds?'

Amanda was cagey. 'Work,' she said simply.

'Which is?' Drake pressed.

'I'm a scientist,' Amanda volunteered, feeling on pretty safe ground. Nine times out of ten, this information killed that particular line of questioning stone dead. She reached into her purse and took out a picture of Emily.

'I'm a mad scientist, and this is my beautiful daughter.'

Drake looked at the picture and smiled. He was the exception. 'As beautiful as her mother. What kind of scientist? My guess would be chemistry. You'd be very good at it.'

Amanda raised one eyebrow. 'Why do you say that?'

Drake looked pleased with himself. He'd led her all the way to the punchline. 'Well, yours is certainly working on me right now.'

Amanda let it pass. She shook her head. 'No, I'm not a chemist.'

'A physicist, then?'

'Here's some physics. A neutron goes into a bar and says, "How much for a beer?" The barman says, "For you, no charge." '

Drake laughed.

'You're not a scientist but you know about science,' said Amanda, curiously.

'I did an engineering degree,' confessed Drake. 'So come on, what *do* you do?'

'Let's say I apply mathematical solutions to the work of various companies and institutions. Basically, I'm a problem solver.'

Drake grinned sheepishly. 'Then we have something in common. I'm a problem creator. Usually for myself.'

'But not this time?'

'No, not this time,' Drake agreed, with a slightly bitter smile. 'This time I seem to have involved NATO and the US military.'

Amanda remembered the American major general at the airbase. It was too much of a coincidence. She regarded Drake curiously. 'You know something about the crash, don't you?'

Drake was rocked. The conversation had suddenly taken a completely unexpected turn from his usual slick chat-up routine. He was making his own connections. The UFO . . . a scientist. It was his turn to be cagey. 'That could depend on what *you* know. Or what you think you know.'

Amanda was silent for a few moments.

'OK, so let's bluff out our hands for a while,' she suggested finally. 'Are we in agreement that neither of us is talking about an ordinary aircraft crash here?'

Drake was nodding his head in agreement, just about to answer when her mobile rang. It was Inspector Boyd.

'You asked me to let you know if we found anything unusual,' he said. 'Well, a motorist brought a man in to the hospital here. Found him lying in the road. Nearly ran him over. And he's suffering from a high-velocity gunshot wound.'

'I'm on my way,' said Amanda.

She stood up and smiled at Drake. 'I'm sorry. I've got to go.'

'It's about the UFO, isn't it?'

Amanda was taken by surprise. 'It might be,' she said, cagily. How much did this man know?

'I've got to come too.'

'What's your stake in this?' she asked.

'All right,' he said finally, giving in. 'I'm pretty

sure that what crashed here was an escape pod of some kind. The original vehicle was shot down by a Tornado F3 over the North Sea at 23.30 hours last night.'

Amanda stared hard at him for a moment. 'Let's go,' she said firmly. The car journey was going to be interesting, she thought.

Although it was a civilian hospital, there was already an RAF presence there. Flight Lieutenant Radcliffe and three armed squaddies guarded the corridor, looking as though they meant business. Just waiting for the top brass to arrive, reflected Drake. But Amanda's M.o.D. security pass got them through into the isolation ward.

Inspector Boyd and the civilian doctor came out to meet them. They looked mistrustfully at Drake.

'He's with me,' explained Amanda.

Boyd frowned. 'Well, as I said, this man was found by a motorist. Seems like he may have been living rough in the woods. We were called because he has what appear to be high-velocity gunshot wounds.'

The doctor broke in. 'You have to realise the man is very sick and delirious. The wound has gone on to give him blood poisoning.'

She led the way past the guards into the isolation ward, finally opening the door of a private room. Terrell lay on a bed, connected up to a drip and looking deathly pale. He was drenched in sweat, his body convulsing sluggishly. A nurse was trying to dress his horribly infected wound.

The doctor barked out her instructions. 'Send cultures. CEF and met. Hourly TPR and blood pressure. And I'd like a portable chest X-ray, please.'

Both Amanda and Drake's first impression was of disappointment, quickly followed by surprise. Apart from these outward symptoms, the patient looked amazingly *normal*, like any other sick man. They exchanged a puzzled glance. The man lying on the bed was not what they had been expecting at all.

His pale lips were moving incessantly, making muted, incoherent sounds. Drake listened intently for a few seconds, looking bemused. If they were words, then they were in no language he had ever heard. He looked up at the doctor.

'What's he saying?'

The doctor shrugged. 'Just gibberish. I told you – he's delirious.'

'What are you doing for him?' Amanda wanted to know.

'We've started a course of antibiotics and taken blood tests to identify the particular germ—'

Amanda didn't give her a chance to finish. 'And was the blood normal?'

The doctor frowned slightly. 'He's mildly anaemic, if that's what you mean.'

Drake shook his head. 'No, what we mean is – was it normal blood? *Human* blood?'

The doctor regarded him with some concern. 'Yes . . .' she said slowly, as if she was talking to an imbecile.

'Well, getting blood poisoning from a high-velocity gunshot wound. Bit unusual, wouldn't you say?'

The doctor smiled patronisingly. 'Uncommon, perhaps. Not unusual.'

Amanda had been taking the opportunity to study the patient more carefully. There was a rash on the backs of his hands and other parts of his body.

'This speckly rash. What is it?'

'Purpura,' the doctor said confidently. 'It's sometimes associated with an infection of this sort.'

Drake had another explanation. 'I've also seen something looking exactly like this on pilots exposed to high G-forces,' he put in. 'Skin capillaries can rupture under sustained accelerations, giving this rash-like appearance. Right, doc?'

The doctor frowned. 'He has a moderate degree of muscle wastage in his body. Higher than one might expect of someone in an active occupation.'

It was the final clue which Drake had been waiting for. 'Weightlessness,' he announced triumphantly, considering his theory proved.

The doctor had heard enough. She had serious doubts over his, and Dr Tucker's official status.

'I'm afraid I'm going to have to ask the military for confirmation of your status,' she informed them both curtly. She stepped to the door, summoning Radcliffe.

'Keep an eye on these two for a moment, will you, Flight Lieutenant.'

'Ma'am.' Radcliffe snapped to attention, taking up a position in the doorway as the doctor left the room.

Drake and Amanda stared over at the pilot, still twitching and muttering feverishly.

'This is a man who's experienced prolonged weightlessness, who's been exposed to high accelerations and who speaks a completely unknown language,' Drake whispered in Amanda's ear. 'The fact that he developed blood poisoning so easily might suggest that he had no immunity from Earth bacteria. I think you've found what you were looking for, don't you?'

There was just one, lingering doubt in Amanda's mind. 'But you just said it yourself – this *man*,' she pointed out. 'He looks perfectly human.'

'But he has to be the one – the one from the UFO,' Drake insisted.

Amanda regarded him curiously. There was still one thing about Drake she didn't quite understand. 'How come you're so eager to believe it?' she asked.

It was time to come clean. There didn't seem to be any point in hiding the truth any longer. 'Because I saw that thing,' Drake said quietly. 'It was like nothing we could build.'

He paused briefly, before the final revelation.

'I was the one who shot him down. They

grounded me for it. That's what I couldn't tell you earlier. Now I've pulled you into the mess I was already in. I'm sorry.'

He turned his eyes to the floor, waiting for her to lash out at him, to hate him for involving her in his trouble: to drop him as quickly as Sarah had done. God, he was good at cocking things up at the moment.

It suddenly occurred to him that he didn't want to cock this one up.

Amanda smiled and shook her head. 'Doesn't matter. Like I said before, I'm good at sorting out messes.'

Drake lifted his head and looked deep into her eyes. He couldn't believe it. She really meant it.

The pilot moaned again. Drake pulled his gaze away from Amanda and looked down at him. He seemed to be becoming slightly more wakeful.

'Who are you?' asked Drake. 'Answer me.'

Terrell continued to moan, rolling over in his agony. Drake was horrified to see the burns and gunshot wound he'd sustained.

'My god,' whispered Drake, sick to the bone. 'I'm so sorry.'

Flanked by Squadron Leader Knox and Wing Commander Friday, Major General Reece regarded Drake and Amanda sourly. The three of them looked like Batman, Batgirl and Robin, Drake thought, struggling to find some humour in the situation.

Reece was anything but humorous. 'Clear the

area of civilians,' he ordered Radcliffe.

He studied Amanda's security pass for a few seconds, then fixed her with a piercing stare. 'Well, Dr Tucker. Something tells me this isn't worth the paper it's printed on. Am I right?'

Amanda said nothing.

Drake spoke up. 'This pilot is a prisoner of war. He should be treated according to the terms of the Geneva Convention.'

'Flight Lieutenant Drake. What a surprise. Any good reason why I shouldn't have you placed under close arrest right now?'

Drake knew there was no way he could make the situation any worse.

'Sir, Dr Tucker intercepted a transmission from the UFO shortly before I shot it down.' He broke off to nod over towards the pilot. 'We believe he was trying to send a message – to his people. There may be others up there.'

To his surprise, Drake realised Major General Reece was actually listening. He cast a sideways, pleading glance at Amanda, looking for back-up.

She was about to speak when Friday interrupted, holding a sheet of exposed film. He seemed flustered. 'Sir, the civilian doctor seems to have missed this. I've found something strange in our pilot's cranial X-ray,' he announced, carrying the film over to a light box on the wall. He waited for everyone to gather round before continuing.

'Here.' Friday tapped the photo with his fingernail. 'There's something small and metallic embedded in his third right upper molar tooth.'

Amanda had pushed past Major General Reece before anyone thought to stop her. She studied the X-ray intently for several moments. 'It's an electronic device,' she said, definitively. 'It could be a micro-miniaturised transmitter of some kind.'

Reece, Knox and Friday exchanged puzzled glances.

Drake had a moment of inspiration. 'Maybe it's a homing device,' he suggested, but no one was listening.

Something was happening. There was a strange noise in the air, starting as little more than the sound of rustling paper but quickly rising to a crackle of intense, building energy. It seemed to be coming from both outside and within the room at the same time. Everyone felt the hair on the back of their necks prickle, as though they were caught in a powerful electrical field. Radcliffe and three of his men rushed into the room, guns drawn.

'What the hell is it? What's going on?'

Knox looked baffled. 'Helicopter?' she suggested weakly.

Radcliffe shook his head. 'That's no helicopter.'

Drake glanced over towards the bed. He grasped Amanda's arm, tugging it insistently. 'Look at him,' he hissed.

Amanda looked. The man had managed to pull himself up against his pillows, despite his weak condition. His face, still flushed with delirium, was contorted into a mask of fear, his eyes wide

and staring. It was obvious that he was terrified.
His lips moved, framing a single word.

'Enemy,' he croaked.

Drake and Amanda exchanged a quick, surprised glance.

'He speaks English,' Drake muttered, voicing
the obvious.

Amanda rushed to the bedside. 'What is it? Is it
your people?' she demanded.

Terrell was convulsed with terror. His head
shook violently from side to side, like a man
gripped by an epileptic seizure. His eyes were
rolling wildly. 'Others,' he managed to grate out.
'Not like us. *Monsters*.'

The crackling had built up to an ear-splitting
crescendo now. Above it, Radcliffe's voice rose in a
scream.

'Christ! What's that?'

Everyone turned in his direction, catching his
point of view. Radcliffe was staring towards the
window, suddenly ablaze with unnatural radiance. The window-frame itself appeared to
expand, contract then expand once more. Its
geometric lines were distorted, becoming a paral-
lelogram, a trapezoid, a rectangle again. Behind
it, fluid, moving shapes appeared, flitting like
shadows, jumping and changing position almost
instantaneously.

'They're coming in,' Radcliffe cried. 'Lay down
suppressing fire.'

The weird light flooded into the room, sear-
ingly white, blinding. The room itself was

changing. The walls buckled, bulged inwards. The ceiling drooped towards the floor, bubbling like melted cheese.

Tuffley opened fire, pumping bullets blindly towards the window, with only the sound of shattering glass to give him direction. Another gun opened up somewhere else in the room, firing sporadically. Someone screamed out in pain.

Above the din, Reece's voice rose in a shout. 'Pick targets, men. Pick targets.'

'We can't see anything!' Tuffley yelled, still firing wildly. A third gun joined the din, adding to the fat sound of bullets smacking into walls. In the total chaos, no one seemed to realise that the blinding light was dying away, the crackling energy sounds diminishing.

'Hold fire!' Radcliffe shouted eventually, but the sound of gunshots continued for at least another five seconds. Then, abruptly, there was a momentary silence, broken finally by Friday's whimpering voice.

'I'm hit, I'm hit.'

The light had returned to normal, but everybody was still dazzled. Drake rubbed at his eyes, straining to get his vision back and take stock of his surroundings. Finally, gradually, he was able to make out the main features of the room and some of its occupants again.

Friday lay sprawled on the floor, half-propped up against one of the walls, the front of his white coat red and sticky with fresh blood. His eyes, wide and glazed looking with shock and disbelief, were fixed on the gory mess.

'I'm hit, I'm hit,' he bleated, repeatedly.

Radcliffe bent over Friday, still moaning. He glanced up at Reece, clearly flustered. 'There's all this blood, but I can't find a wound, sir.'

From his different angle, Drake could see a prone body, half-hidden behind an empty bed. 'That's because it's not his blood,' he muttered. 'There's your victim.'

Radcliffe half-turned, identifying the police inspector who was clearly dead, hit by at least two close-range bullets. One of them had taken him in the back, blowing out through his heart and chest. Radcliffe's eyes met Tuffley's, exchanging a brief and guilty look, knowing that they had shot one of their own men. In his state of shock, the anger flared outward, finding a target in the still whimpering Friday.

He seized the man by the lapels of his coat, shaking him violently. 'It's Boyd's blood, you snivelling git. Boyd, not you.'

'That's enough, Flight Lieutenant,' Reece snapped. He'd seen enough of men under extreme combat stress to recognise the symptoms. They were all shaken and scared. Different men coped with it, or concealed it, in different ways. His was to assume a calm, authoritative position of command. He scanned the room, taking stock.

Amanda and Squadron Leader Knox had both dived for the floor at the first sound of gunfire, and were now climbing to their feet. Reece directed his attention to Sergeant Tuffley. 'Whatever it was has gone.' He paused to nod down at Boyd's body. 'Go find a stretcher and a couple of medics, will you. Get him out of here.'

Tuffley managed a shaky grin of bravado. 'Guess we scared 'em off, eh sir?'

Drake cast him a scathing glance. 'All we managed to do was hit one of our own men.'

'Maybe not,' Amanda murmured, catching their attention. She had approached the shattered window and was inspecting the frame. Partly melted and surrounded by scorch marks, what remained of the surround was covered in deposits of a viscous substance the colour and texture of semi-cold custard.

'This could be their blood,' Amanda mused.

Radcliffe snorted with derision. 'What do you mean, their blood?'

'You think someone popped a zit the size of a football?' Drake asked sarcastically.

Radcliffe bristled. Amanda jumped in quickly. 'Look, you saw them,' she reminded him.

'We don't know *what* we saw,' Reece put in firmly. It was more than a statement, almost a command. He approached Amanda. 'What do you make of these scorch marks? Any theories?'

She fingered part of the melted window frame, which was still hot to the touch. 'A sudden and intense energy release might account for damage like this. It ties in with everything else we saw and heard.'

Drake's eyes fell on the portable X-ray machine

which Friday had brought into the room.

'If there was an emission of energy, wouldn't the X-ray plates have picked up something?' he asked.

Amanda nodded. 'Quite possibly.' She turned to Reece. 'It might be a good idea to get them developed.'

'I'll see to it, sir,' Squadron Leader Knox volunteered. It was a good excuse to get out of the room and have some time to think. She exited, wheeling the X-ray machine.

'What now, sir? Should I call for reinforcements?' Radcliffe asked Reece. He nodded over to the pilot. 'His unit could try to get him back again any time.'

'Not his unit,' Amanda put in. 'The others.'

Reece frowned at her. 'What others?'

'The ones he mentioned?' Drake asked.

Amanda nodded. 'I think so. He tried to send out a transmission – we can only assume to his own people – and then it was blocked, deliberately jammed, by someone else. We have no idea where the second signal came from.'

Drake pointed to the yellow goo on the window-frame. 'It came from wherever *they* came from,' he muttered heavily. He looked up at Reece. 'And if that *is* a homing device in his tooth, they're still getting a signal to home in on.'

'Drake's right,' Amanda agreed with a nod. 'We ought to get it out.' She turned to Friday. 'Could you get me a pair of pliers?'

Friday had picked himself up from the floor

and recovered some of his composure. He looked shocked.

'That's criminal assault,' he complained.

'Maybe you guys should just shoot him again instead,' Drake suggested with heavy sarcasm.

Reece ignored the banter. 'Do it,' he muttered curtly to Amanda. 'On my authority.'

Grudgingly, Friday sought out a pair of surgical pliers and a small specimen pot. He followed Amanda over to the pilot.

She looked at him apologetically. 'I'm sorry, but it's the only way.' She glanced up at Friday. 'Just show me which tooth it is.'

Drake came over to help. He held the pilot's head while Amanda pulled the tooth with cool, clinical precision, ignoring the man's agonised cries of pain. She dropped it into the specimen pot and handed it to Friday.

'I'll have this analysed, sir,' he said to Reece.

Reece snorted. 'Have it *neutralised*,' he snapped. He was silent for several seconds after Friday left the room, regarding Amanda thoughtfully. Finally, he seemed to have come to a decision.

'Dr Tucker, I'd like to have you in on this,' he announced. 'The situation looks to be contained here, so no word gets out.'

'I don't work for the military,' said Amanda levelly, holding his gaze.

But Reece could tell she was obviously interested. Dead interested.

'So you believe us now?' Drake asked, assuming that the offer included him.

Reece glared at him. 'You've got no job here, Drake. Ship out.'

It might be time to make a discreet exit, Amanda thought. 'I ought to have said to do mineralogy on that tooth,' she announced. 'It might tell us more about where he's from.' She left to catch up with Friday, leaving the two men to argue things out.

Friday was about thirty yards down the corridor, now guarded on both sides by numerous armed military personnel. Amanda was about to break into a run to catch him up when something stopped her.

The lines of the corridor didn't look quite true. There was a slight curvature on one side and the opposite wall met the ceiling at the wrong angle. Amanda stopped in her tracks. Perhaps her vision was still impaired, she thought. She blinked her eyes several times before staring ahead once again, expecting the illusion would have cleared. It hadn't.

If anything, the distortion was more pronounced. The left-hand wall had a distinct bulge to it now, and the corridor itself seemed to curve off to the right towards the end. A shiver of apprehension rippled through her body. There was no crackling sound, and yet . . .

She screamed out to Friday. 'Come back – NOW!'

The unearthly light literally burst into the far end of the corridor like a silent explosion. Even where she was, Amanda felt a shock or pressure wave hit her, like a sudden strong gust of wind. Then the energy sound was back, amplified by the enclosing walls into a deafening roar.

Horrified, Amanda watched as Friday was swept up off the floor and lifted into the air. His body seemed to elongate, as though he was being stretched like a piece of soft toffee. Then, feet-first, he was sucked towards the form withering and deflating like a punctured balloon.

Three of the armed guards sprang into attack, dropping to their knees on the floor and opening fire. A trio of separate and distinct laser-like pulses erupted from the general radiance, starting as pencil-thin beams but turning into fat, writhing serpents of radiant energy. Each plucked an airman from his position, distorted him into a cartoon-like caricature of a human body before sucking them away.

Amanda tried to turn and run, but her feet felt as though they were glued to the floor. Petrified with fear, she could only gaze wide-eyed into the brilliance as if hypnotised. Then something dark and huge and shapeless was emerging from the light, moving up the corridor towards her at incredible speed. She screamed.

The sound of gunfire had alerted Reece, who rushed out into the corridor with Drake hot on his heels. There was an overpowering stench of scorched paint and linoleum. They found Sergeant Tuffley, leaning back against one of the walls looking dazed and disorientated.

'Where's Amanda?' Drake demanded.

Tuffley took some time to answer. 'Gone,' he managed to gasp out at last. 'Along with Friday and three of our men.'

Radcliffe had arrived to join them. 'Another attack?' he asked of Tuffley, receiving an affirmative nod. He turned to Reece, looking confused and apologetic. 'I just don't understand how they managed to infiltrate this place, sir. The whole hospital is crawling with armed guards, inside and out.'

Reece hastened to put Radcliffe at his ease. 'No one's blaming you, Flight Lieutenant. We can only assume that the pilot's unit homed in on that device in his tooth.'

'Not his unit,' Drake muttered firmly. 'A *different* alien force, in conflict.'

But Major General Reece had other priorities on his mind. 'Keep out of this, Drake,' he snapped testily. He returned his attention to Radcliffe, rattling off orders in quick-fire succession. 'We transfer at first light. I want a secure holding tank for the prisoner at Field HQ. A full ground force with armour and triple A. Permanent radar surveillance and continuous air patrol. Go.'

'Yes sir.' Radcliffe was away at the run.

It was a natural hiatus. Drake took advantage of it, desperate to get his message across.

'Look, General, you have to understand. There have got to be two extraterrestrial forces at work here. Two – a duality. One half of a ballet dancer's dress. Two.'

Any answer Reece might have given was mercifully curtailed as a member of Friday's medical team approached, silently handing Reece an X-ray envelope. He pulled out the plate and studied it, deliberately holding it away from Drake's viewpoint.

'I take it this is what the machine picked up during the energy burst?' Drake asked.

Reece nodded wordlessly, struck speechless by the weird and scary image on the plate. He was clearly shaken. As if he needed confirmation of his sanity, he let Drake see it.

If nothingness could be isolated and photographed, it would probably look something like this, Drake thought. The energy emission showed up as a radiant, jagged, roughly circular mouth to a vortex, behind which there was only blackness. A gateway, a portal, between reality and whatever lay beyond it. And something, hideously and grossly distorted, was stepping through that portal.

By no possible stretch of the imagination could the grotesque image be called a creature, even vaguely humanoid. Yet its shape, its stance, its implied movement suggested something living, something intelligent, something with a purpose.

'Two forces,' Drake repeated dully, his voice little more than a shocked whisper. 'The ones associated with the captured pilot, and these – the ones he calls *monsters*.'

There was a long silence. Finally, Reece spoke,

his voice temporarily drained of all authority and self-assurance.

'I'm not here to believe or disbelieve, Drake,' he muttered thickly. 'Just to get the job done.' He paused for a brief moment, eyeing Drake thoughtfully. 'All right, you get to stick around,' he conceded eventually. 'But when I say you're out, you're out.'

Drake sighed with relief. 'Thank you, General. Now, what about getting Amanda and the others back?'

Reece had still not recovered his composure. He was used to an enemy he could see, identify, meet on equal terms. What he faced now was completely beyond the scope of his experience, even his imagination.

He regarded Drake blankly. 'From where?' he asked helplessly. 'How?'

CHAPTER FOUR

Amanda was still screaming, her throat already raw and aching. Yet there was no sense of time having passed. Perhaps whatever had taken her had blanked out her conscious memory but not her bodily functions, she rationalised. She fought to control her terror, take stock of her surroundings.

She was comfortably warm, lying in a supine position, but there was no sensation of anything tangible supporting her back. She felt weightless, devoid of sensory input.

She tried to rise, but found that it was impossible. Any attempt to move seemed to propel her body sluggishly in the completely opposite direction, but that movement was then almost immediately cancelled out by some opposing, yet resilient force.

She was floating, she realised, in something viscous, thicker than air and water.

Once, several years ago, she had taken part in a series of experiments with sensory deprivation, which included spending prolonged periods in a sealed, lightproof and soundproof flotation tank filled with a highly saturated solution of epsom salts in water. The experience now was similar, but with one radical difference. In the tank she had floated on the surface; now she was completely immersed, floating *in* the unknown substance rather than upon it. Yet she appeared to be breathing normally. Amanda was baffled.

Also, she could hear. There was a muted pulsing, throbbing sound all around her. For a while, Amanda thought it might be her own heartbeat, but then she realised that the rhythm was slower, and out of synch. Other, more strident sounds occasionally penetrated through, increasing Amanda's sense of fear. Muffled, sometimes distorted in pitch, they were nevertheless clearly identifiable as screams of pain and terror, torn from human throats.

The trick of manoeuvring herself seemed to be in using her own body weight as a counterbalance to any movement she wanted to make, Amanda learned after a few minutes. Finally, as long as she did it very slowly and deliberately, she was able to move her head from side to side and take in her surroundings.

She was contained within a cell-like compartment, which was itself within a much larger, multi-chambered structure. There was not a single geometric shape or plane in sight. Her environment was shapeless, to all intents and purposes completely random in design and construction – yet its overall structure and dimensions appeared to be fluid, distorting, expanding and contracting again with no apparent pattern. The walls – if the leathery confines of her prison could be called that – seemed to have a life of their own, constantly undulating and flexing like muscles. Each movement seemed to be accompanied by a slight secretion of slimy fluid, the colour of pus from an infected wound.

For a while, Amanda considered the fantastic possibility that she had been swallowed by a giant creature. Certainly everything she could see suggested living tissue. She wondered, morbidly, if the yellow secretion might be some kind of digestive juice.

There was a faint plopping sound, and suddenly Amanda was no longer alone. The naked body of a young airman was deposited nearby, apparently out of nowhere. There was something almost mechanical about his sudden delivery. Amanda modified her theory. Not the body of some fabulous beast then, she decided. But a construction, a device of some kind created out of living tissue, rather than brick and steel.

She turned her attention to the young man, recognising him as one of those who had been swept up with Friday. He was no older than nineteen, Amanda estimated. He looked utterly terrified, gaping at her through wide, vacant eyes.

With a great deal of effort, Amanda discovered that she could propel herself towards him. She moved across to his side in a series of small eddies, managing to end up with her face close to his.

Up to that second, Amanda had not considered any problems of communicating in a liquid environment. But if people could scream, then they could also talk, she assumed.

She thrust out her hand, touching the airman's shoulder in what was supposed to be a gesture of comfort. Instinctively, he cringed in fear, bobbing away from her. Amanda tried again.

'It's all right. I'm one of us,' she murmured soothingly. 'I was at the hospital, remember?'

Her voice sounded thick, echoing – but it was clear that the young man could hear her. He nodded faintly, calming slightly.

'SAC Woodward, Tony. Serial number PF 590075,' he muttered back, following strict orders for capture and interrogation.

'I'm Amanda, Tony,' she informed him. 'We need to trust each other if we are to get out of this.'

Terror returned to Woodward's eyes. 'We're never going to get out of this,' he blurted out. 'They're going to kill us.'

Amanda tried to shake her head, but it was just too much effort. 'Listen to me, Tony. We're all going to go home again, I promise. But we have to survive so that we can recount what we learn here. We have to share information, help each other.'

Amanda waited for a few moments to let Woodward calm down again. 'Now take a look around you,' she urged him finally. 'What do you see? What are your impressions?'

'Everything's sort of . . . fleshy,' Woodward said, uncertainly.

'Yes, that's right. So perhaps these creatures have a technology which is based on organic matter. Muscles instead of metal, bone in place of concrete, nerves instead of wires. Do you follow?'

Woodward was hesitant. 'Yes . . . I think so.'

'Good.' Amanda was thoughtful for a while, considering how to phrase her scientific deductions so far in layman's language. It was important that the young airman understood. He might be the only one who got out.

'Now, remember when they took us? That bright light, those crackling sounds? That was energy, Tony. I believe they use a high-mass source of some kind to open a doorway, a portal, into our space.'

Amanda wasn't sure she was getting her message across. Woodward now looked totally confused as well as frightened. 'They're putting things inside our heads,' he whimpered plaintively. 'It hurts to think.'

Amanda grasped his arm, squeezing it tightly. 'You have to fight them, Tony. We both have to fight them. Don't try to think. Just listen to me, all right?'

Woodward appeared to make an effort. 'Yes,' he muttered weakly.

'Now besides the light and the noise, everything became distorted – remember that? The walls of the corridor appeared to bend. I think that means that their power source bends light itself. So that's a sign that they're coming – the walls bend. Got that?'

'The walls bend,' Woodward echoed dully.

Amanda still had no idea how much was actually registering, but she carried on.

'Now what they seem able to do is scientifically impossible in our universe. So somehow they open these portals to bring *their* universe into ours.' Amanda paused. 'Do you understand about dimensions, Tony? The three dimensions of our universe – height, width, depth?'

Woodward was beginning to get stressed again. 'My head hurts,' he moaned again.

Amanda squeezed his arm again, this time in a gesture of comfort. 'OK, Tony – just relax for a while,' she told him. 'I'll talk to you again when you feel better.' She fell silent, reflecting on her own theories thus far.

Spatial dimensions were the clue, she was sure of it. Somehow, these creatures were transposing a fourth dimension into a three-dimensional universe. But then Time was generally considered to be the fourth dimension, and manipulation of time alone would not account for the phenomena.

But supposing there was a *fifth*, even a sixth and seventh dimension, Amanda considered. Even an infinite number of different dimensions, n dimensions, each with different properties and characteristics? Who could possibly know what might then be possible?

She turned her attention back to Woodward. 'How are you feeling now, Tony? Better?'

Woodward opened his mouth to speak. His lips moved, but no sound came out. Then, suddenly, he was gone again.

Alone again, Amanda's terror returned. Perhaps Woodward had been right; they were never going to get out of this alive. An overpowering sense of hopelessness and depression began to settle down upon her like a dark, evil cloud.

Then she remembered her own words to Woodward, just a few minutes earlier. 'We have to fight them, Tony.' Amanda made a supreme effort to rally herself. Perhaps there was no hope, she told herself, facing up to the worst possible scenario. Perhaps she would not get out of this situation alive, or in a fit mental state to recount her observations. But there were other ways that even a body could carry a message – and that message might in turn be the difference between life and death to those on the outside.

Amanda chewed at one of her perfectly mani-cured fingernails with her teeth, splitting it lengthways and sharpening the broken edge to a jagged point. Gritting her teeth against the pain, she began to scratch at the inside of her arm, gouging two simple letters into the soft flesh. nD – infinite dimensions.

Intent on her self-mutilation, her eyes clouded with tears, Amanda failed to notice the manner of Woodward's return. Suddenly he was just there again in the chamber with her, bobbing lightly up and down a few feet away to her left. She paddled her way across to him, comforting words at the ready.

But Woodward was beyond comfort. His eyes, dull and vacant, stared without seeing. Caked and dried blood stained both his ears. There was a shaved patch on the top of his head, and a small, circular section of his skull had been removed, exposing his brain. He was quite dead.

Amanda's shock hardly had time to register. The nearest fleshy wall bulged, a shape forming behind its membraneous surface. It looked like the head of a caterpillar, only enlarged a thousand times, Amanda thought, shuddering. It was hideous. A thick, greenish mucus dripped from its two mandible-like protuberances.

The bulge extended outwards into a tube, stretching towards her. The caterpillar head plopped on to her abdomen, burrowing into the soft flesh. Amanda felt a sharp stab of pain. The thing was piercing her skin with sharp, bony projections, drawing blood.

Amanda began to scream again.

At first light, Drake found himself in a field ambulance speeding along a country road, in contact with HQ via a field radio. True to his word, Major General Reece had let him stick around – for the moment. He'd been put in charge of the prisoner's security during his transfer from the hospital to the air base, under strict orders to shoot the pilot if anyone attempted to abduct him again.

Drake looked down at the injured man. He looked so unthreatening. He was now only slightly delirious, lying there on a stretcher with an intravenous drip in his arm, hooked up to an oxygen and cardiac monitor, an RAF doctor checking the readings. He looked so vulnerable, gripping his cheek where Amanda had pulled the tooth.

Amanda . . .

Drake thought back to the terror that had come over the pilot's face when those other creatures had appeared. Wherever they were, whatever they were, they not only had Wing Commander Friday and three airmen, they'd taken Amanda, too. It suddenly occurred to him that he really cared what happened to her. But it seemed like wherever he went he left a trail of destruction behind him. Everyone involved with him got hurt. He suddenly felt very lonely.

'So who are you?' asked the doctor, conversationally.

Drake woke out of his reverie. He smiled. 'Dental nurse.'

The doctor was about to reply when Drake held up his hand to silence him. Something was coming over the radio. He listened intently. Knox and Reece were worried about something.

'Interceptors airborne to a radar contact.'

'Heading?'

'Inbound.'

'If it fails to identify itself, interceptors will engage and destroy.'

Drake looked up again at the doctor. 'They've got something heading our way.' He listened again. 'Range forty miles and closing.'

Reece and Knox were making another exchange.

'Contact not responding to radio challenge.'

'Engage and destroy.'

'Condor orders engage and destroy.'

'Now twenty nautical miles,' said Drake, trying to keep the tension out of his voice. It was happening again, he thought.

Knox's voice sounded urgent.

'Interceptors have yet to acquire target. Sir, the contact is closing in on us. We've already seen how they can come through our defences.'

'I'm giving the order. Tell Drake.'

'Condor to ambulance . . .'

Drake felt sick to his stomach as Knox's call came through.

'Acknowledge.'

He stood up and drew his pistol. 'Doctor, please step away from the patient.'

The doctor moved aside, horrified, giving Drake a clear target. Drake pointed the pistol at the prisoner's head, meeting the pilot's eyes as he did so. They looked so calm, so infinitely sad – so human. Drake's hand started to shake.

Knox's voice came over the radio again, more insistent this time.

'We know we can't stop them extracting him. We

can't let him be interrogated. Acknowledge!'

Drake remained rooted to the spot, looking into the depths of the pilot's eyes. He remembered how excited and angry he'd felt, chasing the contact up there in the sky, what seemed like a lifetime ago. How reckless he'd been. How trigger-happy. How dismissive of dear, dead Gerry's pleas. How *dangerous*.

Drake knew he wasn't that man any more. He felt responsible for bringing the pilot down in the first place. He'd got him into this mess. Now he was going to have to shoot the man dead in cold blood. And nobody would be able to tell him afterwards that it wasn't all his own doing. He flinched at the prospect of carrying all that extra guilt. If he shot him now, he'd carry the picture of the man's silent eyes to his grave.

'Contact closing. Carry out the order. We can't stop them. Carry out the order.'

Terrell returned Drake's gaze, calmer and stronger than the shaking man. He looked at him with mute and puzzled pleading, glancing at the gun, waiting for the shot to come.

Suddenly, the ambulance screeched to a halt. Drake was sent stumbling forwards as the doors burst open. He winced as the bright light flooded into the darkness, then turned the gun back on the pilot.

The doctor screamed as a single shot rang out. 'No!'

Drake wondered for a split second if he had pulled the trigger without realising it when the doctor fell to the ground, clutching his arm. The shot had come from outside the ambulance – from whatever was waiting to take the prisoner.

Then Flight Lieutenant Radcliffe was jumping into the ambulance, shouting at his own men. 'Hold your fire, damn you! Hold your fire.'

The same instant, Drake heard Reece's voice come over the radio.

'Cease fire!'

'The contact's friendly,' panted Radcliffe. 'It's one of ours.'

Drake was in a daze. He looked round at Radcliffe but continued to hold the gun, still pointing it at the wounded pilot.

'Drake, it's OK,' urged Radcliffe. 'They're on our side.'

Drake dropped to his knees, still shaking. He threw the gun down and put his head in his hands.

'The way we're going, Radcliffe, pretty soon there's going to be no one left on our side.'

CHAPTER FIVE

With the transfer to Field HQ, Reece had set up what was, in effect, a full combat unit. He had also established a comprehensive and fully staffed medical and scientific research unit which would have been the envy of many a smaller hospital.

The pilot was over the worst part of his fever now, and making a good recovery. Although still connected up to an intravenous drip, he was sitting up in his bed and taking a keen interest in everything that was going on around him. It was one-way traffic, however. All attempts at interrogation had so far met with a stubborn silence.

Reece, with Drake accompanying him like a shadow, was trying again.

'Tell us who you are and what you're doing here,' Reece demanded.

'Charles Terrell,' answered the pilot, crisply.

Reece frowned. 'Are you the sole pilot of the vehicle we recovered, or are there others?'

The pilot regarded him stoically. Looking on,

Drake sensed a weariness, rather than defiance, in his expression. He tried a different tack.

'You were brought up on Earth, weren't you?' he asked, in a gentler tone. 'Answer us.'

'Charles Terrell,' repeated the pilot, but Drake was sure he had seen his eyes flicker.

Reece had seen it too. 'If you're military, you know the drill,' he snapped. 'Name, rank, serial number. It's your duty. You can't withhold them.'

A thin, vaguely sardonic smile curved the pilot's lips. 'These questions,' he murmured. 'So pointless. What you or I say or do is of absolutely no importance in what's about to happen to all of us.'

Reece produced the X-ray photograph of the portal opening. He thrust it under the pilot's eyes. 'You mean this?' he demanded. 'You know what this is, don't you?'

Terrell's face registered revulsion, hatred and fear all at the same time. He turned his head, looking away.

'I can't answer,' he said quietly. It sounded almost like an apology.

Reece sighed with exasperation. He looked across the room, out through the glass partition of the medical wing to where Squadron Leader Knox was waiting with two armed guards. Perhaps she would have better luck, he thought, nodding for her to come in and take over. He turned away from the pilot without another word, Drake close on his heels.

'Look, General – there's got to be a reason why he's holding back,' he muttered quietly, as soon as they were safely on the other side of the partition.

Reece scowled. 'If he's a traitor, then he's got a reason,' he said flatly.

Drake shook his head. 'No. It's got to be something else. I can sense it.' He fell silent, listening to Knox's style of interrogation.

Her voice was strident, threatening. 'We want answers, and we will get them out of you,' she informed the pilot. 'You can make it easy on yourself and tell us right now. What is your mission here? Who sent you? What were you sent to do?'

The pilot said nothing. Knox cast a quick, commanding glance to one of the guards, who stepped forward smartly and smacked the back of his hand across the pilot's face.

Outside, Drake flinched, looking at Reece with undisguised disgust. 'Sir, is this really necessary?'

Reece faced him squarely. It was clear that he took no pleasure in what was going on, either. It was a necessary evil. 'We don't know where they're coming from, how many of them there are, or what their purpose is,' he muttered heavily. 'We can't track them, we can't stop them. We've got to know. You tell me if we've got a choice.'

And there was Amanda and the others to get back, Drake thought. He said nothing as Reece walked away, looking back through the partition.

'I've not been taken in like some of the others,' Knox was going on. 'I know what your orders are. You *are* British, aren't you?'

'I'm under orders!' cried Terrell.

'You're an agent of a foreign power plotting to break UK Air Defence. The others might baulk at the treatment you're getting, but me – I've no sympathy for a traitor.'

She stepped back, a cue for another hard slap around the face for the pilot.

If I hadn't shot him down, if it had happened the other way around, that would be me in there now, thought Drake. There had to be another way. A better way.

He went away to find it.

Less than an hour later, Drake was more confused than ever. Radar had picked up another signal near the small town of Kirkhaven, and Squadron Leader Knox had insisted upon a regiment being sent out to investigate.

Drake looked round the Chinook at the other men. Boys laughing and joking with each other, sitting there in combat gear with helmets and camouflage looking forward to a bit of action – they really had no idea what they were up against. A bunch of lads on a jolly day out.

A few days ago, he would have been one of them too. But youth's arrogant belief that you were immortal – that seemed like a lifetime ago. He caught Radcliffe's eye.

'Don't be a shrinking violet, Drake. Introduce yourself to the lads.'

Radcliffe paused. A badly disguised smirk crossed his face.

'Flight Lieutenant Drake here thinks we're fighting little green men!'

The regiment burst out laughing.

'Phone home!' grimaced Tuffley.

Radcliffe hooted with laughter. 'Take me to your leader . . .'

Drake couldn't hold it in any more.

'I guess you gentlemen must be pretty good at bringing in downed pilots. God knows I've reason to be thankful. But you don't seem to understand what it is that we're up against. We're facing an enemy that no one's seen; we don't know their armaments, their objectives – they just came through our defences and took our people. No one could stop them and no one could track them. No one could bring them down.'

He paused, trembling with the force of his anger.

'I just hope we'll all be as *cocky* as this at the end of the day.'

Drake fiercely stared the men out as the Chinook landed, challenging them to find him ridiculous again. All eyes were fixed firmly on the ground. They weren't laughing any more.

Radcliffe was furious. Drake had really got his goat now. But there would be time for all that once the signal had been investigated.

The helicopter had brought them to the lap of a

deep valley covered with the ever-present purple heather so typical of the Scottish countryside. A few tumble-down walls and a rickety old barn were all that were left to show that a small farm had once been here.

Drake ran over to Radcliffe as a message came over the field radio. Radcliffe turned pointedly away and spoke to Tuffley.

'Radar had a fleeting contact. Now they're calling it a *ghost*.' He paused. 'Fan out. Secure the perimeter.'

Sergeant Tuffley barked orders at his men as they spread out across the farm. He took a small squad and started to make his way gingerly towards the barn: the only hiding-place for miles around. If there was a contact, it had to be here.

'Jesus!' cried Tuffley.

A blinding light appeared from nowhere, dazzling the soldiers.

'What the hell's happening?' shouted Radcliffe.

The lines of the barn seemed to be bending – shimmering and unsteady, glowing with an unearthly yellow light. The noise was unbearable: a crackling, harsh, deafening burst of energy.

But above the barn was most terrifying of all. A huge, bright mass of light had appeared, shapeless and shifting; fluid yet somehow solid. A bright flare of nothingness so profound it was painful to look at.

'Pull back!' cried Radcliffe.

Tuffley and his men didn't need telling twice.
'Fire at will!'

A volley of shots rang out as the soldiers fired on the huge mass. But the brilliant light was blinding them: nobody could see to hit anything.

'The barn – mortar fire,' Radcliffe bellowed at his NCOs. 'The UFO – rocket!'

'It's not a UFO,' shouted Drake. 'It's a portal, like they tried to take Terrell with!'

He watched, aghast, as one of the NCOs rigged up a mortar and another loaded up a rocket. What if . . .

'No! There could be our men in there – Amanda!'

Drake started to run towards the barn, eyes averted, hands shielding his face from the glare.

'Drake!' roared Radcliffe. 'Drake!'

But there was no stopping him.

'Hold fire!'

Radcliffe jumped up and set off after Drake. Whatever the crazy son-of-a-bitch was up to, he couldn't let him go in there to face . . . to face his fears alone.

The two men entered the ramshackle barn together, covering for each other as they moved through. The yellow radiance was seeping through the cracks in the wooden walls, still blinding them.

Then it was gone, as suddenly as it had appeared. Drake and Radcliffe flinched, struggling to get used to the darkness.

Radcliffe grimaced. There was yellow slime

everywhere – just like in the hospital when they'd taken the men.

And there in the corner, naked and trembling in the gloom, were Wing Commander Friday and Airmen Miles and Burton.

'Amanda . . .' whispered Drake. But she was nowhere to be seen.

Back at the base the men were soon under observation in the medical wing. Drake stole a glance at Reece and Knox as they watched them through the glass window from the corridor outside. They were horrified. The men looked blank; like zombies or shop dummies, staring straight in front of themselves; motionless, expressionless. They had literally been shocked out of their wits.

Radcliffe leaned in towards Drake.

'Chris, I didn't want to say in front of the men . . . I didn't believe a word you'd said. It just didn't make sense, even after what I'd seen at the hospital. But now . . .'

Drake nodded his head, appreciating Radcliffe's honesty. He understood. It still didn't make sense to him, either.

Through the window, they could see Flight Lieutenant Stewart move towards Miles with a syringe. As he crossed the airman's field of vision, Miles lurched away violently, sobbing and screaming.

'No!'

Major General Reece tapped the glass enquiringly. Stewart looked up and shook his head.

Reece sighed and turned to Knox.

'Get the full story as soon as they're fit. We've got to know more than they've given us so far.'

Knox was astonished. 'You don't believe their stories, do you, General? Spaceships, aliens, medical experiments? I don't believe a word of it, but I believe they do. They've been brainwashed, there's no question about it. And the people responsible are right here on Earth.'

Knox paused, trying to gauge Reece's frame of mind.

'You know, General, given the time, given the right techniques, you can make a man believe almost anything.'

Drake broke in. 'With respect, ma'am, you didn't see what we did.'

Knox snorted. 'If you're right, Drake – and I contend that you are deeply in error – they seem somewhat *limited* for a cosmic power. This time we had them on radar.'

Drake was unmoved. 'I don't think they'd let us pick up their signals unless they wanted us to. They've deliberately delivered our people back to us, and it's got to be for some purpose or other. Sir. Ma'am.'

Drake and Radcliffe departed, leaving Reece and Knox to digest Drake's last remark. They stared through the window in silence for a few minutes more.

'Sir,' began Knox.

'What is it?'

'Sir, I believe I've carried out all your orders so far.'

'You have.'

'Then when are we going to report that we've got Terrell?' she burst out.

Reece was silent.

'When are we going to release our reports on his aircraft? Sir, when are we going to answer our superiors who are questioning why we're—'

Reece was grateful for the interruption as Radcliffe came running back.

'They've found her, sir. Amanda Tucker. She's been picked up safe and sound about two hundred miles south. They're bringing her in right now.'

'Get her into medical as soon as she arrives,' ordered Reece.

'Yes, sir.' Radcliffe headed off.

Reece looked at Knox. She was still waiting for answers.

'I need time, Helen. I need time to prove this thing one way or the other.'

Knox held her breath for a few seconds and looked at her shoes. 'And what if you're wrong, sir?'

CHAPTER SIX

Drake awoke at first light. He dressed hurriedly, eager to see Reece and find out if there had been any news about Amanda. Sergeant Tuffley accosted him as he stepped into the corridor.

'They've found Dr Tucker. She's been brought to the medical wing. General Reece wants you to report to him there.'

Drake nodded, relief flooding his face. 'Thanks.' He set off at a run.

Reece and Knox were outside the wing, looking in through the glass partition. Reece half-turned as Drake joined him.

'She was found wandering aimlessly on a public highway some two hundred miles south of here. They brought her in during the night. She appears to have no recollection of what happened to her.'

'But she's all right?' Drake asked, a little breathlessly.

'See for yourself,' Reece offered, nodding towards the glass. 'She appears in good health, apart from some odd wounds on her arm in the shape of two letters. Small n, big D. She's undergoing a full medical examination right now.'

Drake looked in. Amanda lay propped up in bed, attended by a trio of medical orderlies. As Reece had said, she appeared to be healthy, if a trifle pale. She was also unnaturally calm and placid. Drake assumed they had sedated her.

She looked so small and frail. He wished he could talk to her.

Knox was saying something to Reece.

'Sir, those wounds on Dr Tucker's arm. Our medical team found samples of her own blood and tissue under her fingernails. It would appear that she inflicted those markings on herself – possibly in an attempt to get a message out, even if they killed her. The letters nD: they must mean something.'

Drake winced.

Reece was impressed. To do that to yourself – to be that clear-sighted . . . He whistled softly through his teeth.

'Now where's a woman like that been all my life?' he murmured.

A ghost of a smile flickered across Knox's lips. 'In kindergarten, mostly.'

' "nD",' pondered Reece.

Something clicked in Drake's mind. Scientist . . . science.

'n dimensions,' he burst out. 'More than our conventional three. Amanda must have found evidence that Terrell's enemies make use of higher dimensions of space.'

Knox tutted impatiently.

'Where did you get this from, Drake?' said Reece, sharply.

'I'm a frustrated genius, sir,' retorted Drake, impatiently. 'Look, Terrell was definitely trying to tell his people something. That's why the others – these creatures of n dimensions – nDs – wanted him. He's holding back for a reason.'

'Leave it to me,' said Reece.

Drake was insistent. 'Sir, there may only be a short time before they attempt to take him again. I've got to try to get him to talk.'

'No.'

Drake spoke with the anger of desperation. 'With respect, sir, if I'd followed your orders before, Terrell would be dead now. Just like if I hadn't shot him down, we'd never have got this chance.'

It was Reece's turn to get angry. 'We had a deal. You're only here on my say so.'

'Fine,' shouted Drake. 'I request a board of enquiry be reconvened—'

Reece shouted back. 'You disobeyed a direct order—'

'—to exonerate my actions and return me to flying duties—'

'—and the result of your recklessness—'

'—so I can be up there ready for them—'

'—was the death of your navigator.'

Drake flinched like he'd been shot. He turned on his heel and walked away.

Radcliffe was guarding Terrell when Drake arrived.

The pilot was in bad shape. His lower lip looked red and painful, one of his eyes was puffy and the blue discolouration of bruising was beginning to appear over his right cheekbone. He looked up at Drake.

'So now it's your turn,' he muttered thickly.

Drake shook his head. 'It's not what you think. My name is Christopher Drake. I've come to tell you something.'

'Hang on a minute,' interrupted Radcliffe. 'Have you okayed this with General Reece?'

'If anyone asks, I told you I had.'

Radcliffe shook his head. 'Chris—'

Drake's eyes were urgent, pleading.

'You were up at the farm. You saw. You know what we're up against. Please, Jim.'

Radcliffe looked at him. He closed his eyes and let out a sigh.

'Thanks,' whispered Drake.

Terrell's eyes betrayed a flicker of interest as Drake turned back to him.

'We've met before,' he went on.

The pilot looked curious. 'You have me at a disadvantage.'

'Not on the ground,' Drake said. He jabbed his finger at the ceiling. 'Up there. I'm the reason you're here.'

'Ah.' Terrell nodded faintly, understanding. He seemed to sense that this interrogation would be different. He managed a brief smile. 'I intended no threat, you know.'

'I wasn't to know that. I'm sorry. I thought I was doing the right thing. Perhaps if our roles had been reversed, if it had been the other way around – well, maybe you'd have done the same.'

Terrell nodded again. 'Perhaps I would,' he conceded. He paused. 'Were you injured?' he asked finally.

'My nav was killed,' Drake said flatly.

Terrell looked genuinely distressed. 'I'm sorry,' he said. 'For anyone to be harmed was quite the last thing I wanted.'

Drake found that he believed the man. 'It wasn't your fault.'

Terrell seemed gratified. 'Thank you. And why are you now posted here?'

'Chris,' said Radcliffe.

Drake ignored him. 'I've been grounded.'

The statement evoked a wry grin. 'I too.'

Drake smiled. They had established a common bond. 'I miss it a great deal,' he confessed. 'Some days, we'd top out over cloud, clear blue sky, only a little chatter coming over the radio. So peaceful.'

Terrell nodded. There was a sad, faraway look in his eyes. 'You should see what it's like up there. Silent. Beautiful. No wind, no gravity. It feels like . . . home.'

Drake felt for him. 'Do you think you will ever see home again?' he asked gently.

Terrell shrugged. 'I can hope.'

'And what about my home?' Drake wanted to

know. 'Are we in danger? When this is all over, will there be a home left for me to go back to?'

Terrell's face clouded over. 'I don't know,' he said regretfully. 'I truly don't. But again, I hope.'

Drake was silent and thoughtful for a while.

'Look, Charles, I'm sorry about your capture,' he said finally. 'It was unplanned, and that's down to me. But I want some good to come out of it, and I hope that you do, too. If we are in danger, and you bring some kind of a warning – why won't you speak to us?'

The man's face betrayed some private, inner turmoil. 'Please, don't press me. I can't say.'

He was nearly there, Drake thought, with a rising sense of frustration. He was so very nearly there. There had to be some way of getting through.

'All right. No more questions. Just listen to me,' he said eventually. 'I think I understand your mission. Your people are at war with another species, and that war has encroached upon Earth without your intention. You were sent here as an observer, weren't you?'

There was no reply, but Terrell's silence was an answer in itself. With a surge of elation, Drake realised that he was getting somewhere at last.

'Who are you working for? Who are the others? Why did they take our people?'

Terrell remained silent.

Drake sat back. 'I must be the world's worst interrogator. I come in here to get you to talk and end up revealing our ignorance instead.'

A smile passed over Terrell's face.

'Chris, I think that's enough,' warned Radcliffe.

'Bear with me. Please, Jim,' begged Drake.

He turned back to Terrell. 'The others – they think you're a traitor, in the service of another air force. But I know you're not. You're not that kind of man. I think that what brought you here is something far, far bigger than petty national rivalries.'

The pilot nodded. 'Yes,' he said, troubled.

'And you were in reconnaisance. You're here purely as an observer – that's why you can't talk to us, isn't it? You're observing the Earth; you and the extraterrestrials whose service you're in?'

'Yes, yes,' admitted Terrell. He was getting more agitated now.

'We're in danger from the others, the ones who use higher dimensions. Aren't we?'

'I can't answer,' cried Terrell. He paused, to look Drake straight in the eye. 'You came here because you need to know something for yourself. You want to know if all this is your fault – whether any of it would be happening if you hadn't shot me down.'

Drake was momentarily stunned, realising that the tables had been turned on him. He stood face to face with his own, true motives for the first time.

'Chris, he's playing mind games with you,' said Radcliffe.

'You see, for my part, I don't know,' Terrell continued. 'I don't know either. If I'd done differently, would all this never have happened? I don't know. If I had acted differently, would anything be changed, could any of this have been avoided?'

He fell silent again, his face impassive. It was obvious that he was not willing to expand any further.

Radcliffe intervened. 'That's it, Chris. I'm putting a stop to this.'

Drake hesitated, as if he was going to speak again.

'Leave it, mate,' urged Radcliffe.

Drake ignored him.

'Help me to understand,' he pleaded. 'You're holding back and I don't know why. I don't understand how any reason could be big enough. How can you stand back and watch this happen – watch it happen to your own planet, your own people?'

A look of anguish crossed the pilot's face, but he remained silent. Drake's shoulders slumped, as he resigned himself to failure. He turned away.

He was almost out of the door when Terrell spoke again. 'Charles Terrell. Lieutenant, British Army. 520699.'

CHAPTER SEVEN

Early next morning, Drake was standing in the corridor of the medical wing in a world of his own, watching Amanda through the window as she underwent more tests under hypnosis. She spoke as if she was in a dream.

'I had something to tell Wing Commander Friday. I was trying to catch up with him. Then . . . nothing.'

'You must tell us, Amanda. You've got to tell us,' urged Reece.

'I have no memory,' she insisted. 'There's nothing. Then the road, then being picked up by the lorry. I'm lost, not clear where I am.'

'What did they do to you?' demanded Reece.

'I don't remember.'

'Do they have a purpose for you? Tell us,' he entreated.

Amanda lapsed into silence.

Drake stared at her, so lost, so silent. He jumped, startled, as he heard Major General Reece's voice in his ear.

'Come,' he muttered. 'I want you to see the others.'

Reece led the way down to the room next to Terrell's. He opened the door, stepping in with Drake at his heels.

Wing Commander Friday and Airmen Miles and Burton were in three adjoining beds, sharing two orderlies between them. Unlike Amanda, they were all far from placid; tossing fitfully, making occasional moaning sounds, as though they were in the grip of a waking nightmare.

Squadron Leader Knox was already in the room, standing beside Burton's bed. She glanced up, acknowledging Reece and Drake.

'I'm afraid we're not getting much, sir,' she apologised. She turned her attention back to Burton.

'I want you to tell me again about these medical tests,' she said.

The young airman's eyes rolled wildly. There was a nervous twitch pulling at the corner of his mouth. His voice came in little gasps, as though he could hardly catch his breath.

'They stuck things in us . . . probes. In our ears, heads. Injections.'

'Who were *they*?' Knox demanded. 'Which country were they from?'

Burton threshed on his bed. 'Not . . . people,' he hissed.

'You must have seen signs, notices, even medical notes,' Knox pressed. 'What language were they written in?'

The airman stiffened, suddenly. His body began to convulse. Within seconds he was in the throes of what looked like an epileptic fit. A froth of saliva bubbled from his mouth, his eyes glazed over. Every extremity was trembling violently.

Knox stepped smartly back from the bed as one of the orderlies rushed over to administer an anti-convulsant injection. Seeing the needle, Burton's voice rose in a loud, piercing and anguished scream. 'No!'

Knox's shoulders slumped. She turned away from the bed as the orderly fought to restrain his patient. She walked slowly over to Major General Reece, a look of total frustration on her face.

'They're all the same,' she said wearily. 'They've been so thoroughly conditioned that if we try to question them in any depth, they just go into a violent seizure. Whoever did this is an expert in advanced brainwashing techniques.'

'But Dr Tucker is different,' Reece mused. 'Why?'

'Perhaps because she's a woman?' Drake suggested.

Reece shook his head. 'No, I don't buy it. But there's got to be some reason. Maybe her medical examination will throw something up.'

Knox hesitated. 'She may appear normal now – but there's no way of knowing if she will start behaving like the others. It could be a delayed reaction in her case, in which case she should be confined and guarded.'

Reece nodded his head, accepting the truth in Knox's suggestion but not totally happy about it. 'We need her expertise,' he pointed out.

'Suppose we just assign someone to watch over her,' Drake suggested. 'Someone like me, for instance.'

Reece looked dubious. 'And if she starts going crazy on us? You'd pull the trigger?'

It wasn't a question Drake wanted to answer. They both knew the score on that one.

'It should be me,' he insisted, quietly. 'I know her best.'

Reece gave in with a faint shrug of his shoulders. 'OK – until further notice, you've got yourself a job. But your loyalty is to me, not to her – is that clear?'

Drake nodded. 'Perfectly, General.'

'All right. She'll be confined to the med wing until tomorrow morning but, after that, she's your reponsibility.'

Amanda's room was curtained off. Drake assumed that her medical was still in progress. Much as he wanted to talk to her, he guessed it would have to wait a bit longer.

'Has she asked for anyone?' he said hopefully to the soldier on guard outside.

'Just her daughter. She's on the phone to her now.'

Disappointed, Drake retraced his steps back to the main administration block, heading for the computer room.

It was already occupied by Radcliffe, who regarded him with mild curiosity. 'You seem to have your fingers in a lot of pies, Drake,' he observed. 'Looking for something?'

Drake evaded a direct answer, nodding across at the banks of computers. 'Know your way around this gear then, do you?'

Radcliffe shrugged. 'Some of it. Why?'

It was cards on the table time, Drake decided. 'I want to check out Terrell's serial number.'

Radcliffe whistled. 'You and me both. I'm running it at the moment. Here it comes.'

Both men raced over to the printer as it whirred into life. Drake got there first.

He studied the brief details on the computer print-out, shaking his head in complete bewilderment. Nothing made sense. He'd really thought, in those last few moments with the pilot, that he'd got through to the man, established trust, arrived at the truth. And now this. He read the message yet again, hoping there was some hidden clue, something he'd missed.

Terrell, Charles Edward Henry. Lieutenant. Royal Engineers. Assigned to bomb disposal. Born November 13, 1901. Received commission August 1943. Reported missing October 1944.

Drake ripped the sheet out of the feeder with an anger borne of frustration and his own impetuosity. That single page of computer print-out was all he had to show for his unauthorised interrogation, and it wouldn't be enough to save him from the inevitable fallout if and when Knox and Reece found out.

He pulled the original print-out from his pocket, offering it to Radcliffe.

Radcliffe scanned the brief message quickly, as a disbelieving frown appeared over his face. 'Born 1901? Looks like he's led you up the garden path on this one.'

Drake looked suitably sheepish. 'Yeah, probably. But is there any way of checking this info out? A service record?'

'Come on, mate, it's already bad enough you fell for it,' said Radcliffe.

'Please, Jim.'

Radcliffe thought about it for a moment. 'I'll have a look. I could possibly pull a picture out, if it survived the war,' he conceded. 'And if it was genuine,' he added quickly, covering himself.

'Would you?' Drake asked. 'You see, I can't figure out why he would give the name of an officer who disappeared over fifty years ago. There must be hundreds of more recent missing-in-actions he could have used who'd be a lot more credible.'

True enough, but Radcliffe had an answer. 'They'd also be a lot easier to check out,' he pointed out. 'If this guy is just trying to cloud the issue, he's going the right way about it.'

'Try it, will you?' Drake urged. 'And the photograph, if there's one on file.'

Radcliffe gave a sceptical grin. 'Well, I don't see the point, but I'll give it a go.' He moved over to the computer keyboard, tapping out an entry code. After a moment, he looked up, surprise on his face. 'There *is* something in the records. It's coming up now,' he announced.

Drake hurried over, studying the computer screen intently as the message finally came up.

Terrell, Charles Edward Henry. Lieutenant. Temporarily removed from bomb disposal in August 1944. Assigned to Special Duties (information restricted). Reported AWOL October 26, 1944. Charged in his absence with desertion. Case never closed.

Drake blew his breath out through his teeth. 'Now what the hell does that mean?'

Radcliffe had a slightly triumphant grin on his face. 'What it means, mate, is that our man, or his bosses, are a lot cleverer than we gave them credit for. He's managed to find himself an ID and a cover story which is completely untraceable.'

'No, you misunderstood my question. I meant, what were these "special duties" they mention?' Drake said. 'Why "restricted information"? What were the exact circumstances of his disappearance, and why all the mystery?'

Radcliffe grinned again. To him, the answers seemed obvious. 'Well, the fact that he was in bomb disposal probably means the guy was a bit of a headcase to start with. "Special duties" is probably a neat little Army euphemism for saying he was off with the shrinks for a while without it spoiling his service record. Looks to me like he lost his bottle, did a runner and probably spent the rest of the war hiding out under a mattress in Barnsley.'

Drake smiled despite himself. Then, across the room, the printer whirred into life again.

'What's that?' he asked.

'There was a photo available, so I called it up,' Radcliffe told him. 'That should settle the matter once and for all.'

He walked over to the machine as it finished printing, picking up the single sheet of paper and turning it face up. The grin faded from his face. Wordlessly, he handed the sheet to Drake.

The picture was black and smudgy – a bad reproduction of what had obviously been a poor quality black-and-white photograph to start with. It showed the face of a man, in his early forties, wearing the cap of a British Army Lieutenant.

It was also quite unmistakeably the face, perhaps aged four or five years at the moment, of the man lying in bed in the medical wing no more than two hundred yards away – yet it was time, rather than distance, that separated them, made it impossible for them to be one and the same.

'Perhaps he had a son, a kid brother maybe,' Radcliffe suggested, finally finding his voice.

Drake shook his head slowly. Against all logic, he could only believe the evidence of his own eyes, and a deep feeling of intuition in his gut. He wasn't sure why, and he certainly didn't know how, but he knew with absolute certainty that Charles Terrell and the pilot were one and the same man.

He also knew that Major General Reece wasn't going to like it.

CHAPTER EIGHT

'The Lorentz transformation,' Amanda said confidently. She lay back in her hospital bed, propped up against a thick wadge of pillows. Apart from her bandaged arm, she looked fine.

Reece and Knox gaped at her blankly. The phrase meant nothing to any of them. Drake, however, looked interested.

'It's an extrapolation from Einstein's Theory of Relativity,' Amanda explained. 'Named after the mathematician who developed it. Here, I'll show you.' She reached for the pencil and note-pad on her bedside table and scribbled something down, handing it to Reece.

He studied the equation for some time, still not understanding.

$T' = t \times \tilde{A}(1 - v2/c2)$

'Basically, it says that at relativistic speeds, time travels more slowly,' Amanda went on. 'The closer you approach the speed of light, the less time passes subjectively. So Terrell could have been travelling in space and aged only a few years, while here on Earth more than half a century has gone by.'

Squadron Leader Knox snorted in disgust. 'More science-fiction stories,' she scoffed. She stared hard at Amanda. 'No one disputes Einstein's Theory of Relativity, Doctor. I do, however, dispute your and Drake's Theory of Terrell.'

Drake ignored her, addressing himself to Major General Reece instead.

'I think it's pretty clear, sir. Terrell was taken among the Echoes in 1944 and has been returned by them now as an observer.'

'Echoes?' Reece asked, puzzled by the reference.

'Extraterrestrials of unknown origin. EUO – Echo Uniform Oscar,' Drake explained. 'For want of a better title.'

Knox rolled her eyes in an expression of complete and utter disgust. 'My God, you're even giving them names now. Can't we all stay on Earth and see this thing for what it really is? This photograph of Terrell could have been planted in the records. If it is genuine, then the man we have purporting to be Terrell could be a descendant, a double, or an imposter who has undergone plastic surgery. Whatever, his cover story merely serves as a further distraction to our discovering his true identity, country of origin and his military mission here.'

She broke off to cast a despairing look at Reece. 'Sir, you don't believe one word of this, do you?'

Reece said nothing, but the troubled look on his face showed that he was about ready to be convinced. It was the final straw for Knox. With a final glare at Amanda and Drake, she stormed out of the room.

Drake took the opportunity to put the pressure back on Reece. 'Sir, Terrell has warned us – we're in great danger from the others, these nDs. Isn't it about time we opened this thing up to the rest of the military?'

Reece sighed heavily. 'Suppose, just suppose, that you and Dr Tucker are right,' he muttered. 'I'm not saying you are, because nobody can yet, but just suppose. Right now my job is containment, figuring out why they're here, of all places, and what they want. This thing could blow up in our faces any time – but I'm out on a limb. Aliens, other dimensions . . . who's going to believe us?

Amanda thought he had missed a rather important point, and said so. 'Meanwhile, General, they could appear in any place, any country, at any time. I believe that the way these creatures use and travel in higher dimensions of space means that they can materialise anywhere they choose.'

'And we have no way of predicting when and where they might appear?' Reece asked.

'Not at the moment, other than the early visual clue that surrounding objects become distorted. However, that in itself suggests that light is being bent, which would require stupendous amounts of energy. I believe we might be able to develop detectors which would give at least a few seconds of warning about such a build-up.'

There was just one point which Drake didn't understand. 'So if they use all this energy, where do they get it from?'

Amanda hunched her shoulders. 'I don't have a clue. I can only assume they have some way of transporting it with them. What the original source is remains anyone's guess.'

Reece had taken all this on board. He sucked at his teeth thoughtfully. 'So, the bottom line is, you're telling us that we currently have no way of knowing when they will break through and no way of neutralising them. And we've already found out to our cost that we can't stop them when they get here. Is there any good news?'

'Only their limitations,' Amanda said calmly. 'As I said, these "portals" they open into our time and space require massive amounts of energy. Obviously, the more matter you transfer through such a portal, the more energy it takes and the less stable the opening is. So the more they want to bring through, the less time they have.'

'Which in real terms, means what?' Reece demanded.

'For the present, at least, they're stuck with small, temporary portals they can only use for short periods of time to bring through strictly limited amounts of materials or personnel. From a military point of view, I'd say they're probably incapable of launching a mass attack.'

As good news, it carried a sting in the tail which Reece couldn't possibly miss.

'You say "for the present". Are you telling me that this situation could change?'

Amanda shook her head. 'I honestly don't know, General. Until I can get out of this bed and do some serious calculations and computer simulations, I'm merely theorising.'

'For someone who is only theorising, you seem to have got a handle on this thing real easily,' Reece said.

It was a compliment, and Amanda took it as such. She managed a faint smile. 'It's what I do for a living,' she said simply. She paused. 'Which brings me to my question – when can I get back to work?'

Confronted with the direct question, Major General Reece seemed a little awkward. 'That's really down to the medics,' he said, evasively. 'They say you're physically fit enough, but they're a little worried about your apparent lack of memory. Possible evidence of post-traumatic shock, or so they tell me.'

Amanda smiled at him. 'I'm fine, really,' she assured him.

Drake thought, suddenly, of Burton screaming at the sight of a needle, going into a convulsive seizure. And here was Amanda, calm, matter-of-fact, acting as though nothing untoward had happened. Perhaps amnesia was a blessing in her case; but then thinking about it, he had the strangest feeling that her very calmness was somehow *deliberate*, forced. He recalled their first meeting in the pub. The way she had played mind games with him, easing information out of him whilst concealing her own. He sought direct eye contact.

'Is there nothing you can remember at all?' he asked her.

Amanda shook her head. 'Only running after Friday to tell him about the tooth. Then . . . nothing, except vague impressions of being on a road, feeling lost, seeing a lorry. Then being brought back here.'

It was exactly what she'd said under hypnosis.

She broke away from Drake's piercing stare, turning her attention to Reece again. 'But I *do* remember how to do my job,' she said pointedly. 'And how important it is that I get on with it.'

It was a point Reece didn't need reminding about. He needed her desperately and he knew it. 'I'll see what I can do,' he promised Amanda.

He turned back to Drake. 'I'm going to the lab to see if they've turned anything up yet. Want to come along?'

Outwardly, it was an innocent enough invitation, but Drake read a lot more into it and surged with pride. Reece had finally fully accepted him: he was no longer an outsider. It was an important breakthrough.

'Yes, sir, I would,' he said, trying to hide his elation. He followed Reece towards the door, unable to resist turning briefly to flash Amanda a knowing wink. Just for a second, he thought he caught a flash of something akin to guilt on her face, but it was gone before he could identify it.

Reece had come to a decision. 'If I take any longer over trying to convince my superiors . . . I want you on the team, Drake. I regret my earlier remark about what happened to your navigator.'

Drake was momentarily taken aback, but rose to the occasion. 'I apologise for my insubordination, sir. It won't happen again.'

The moment was gone when Radcliffe accosted them in the corridor outside. 'Excuse me, sir,' he said, addressing Reece, 'but Wing Commander Friday is requesting immediate 24-hour compassionate. His wife has been taken ill.'

Reece's brow creased. 'Has he been declared medically fit?'

'Sir, he's still chief MO,' Radcliffe pointed out. 'He's declared himself fit. What should I do, sir?'

Reece deliberated for a few moments. Technically, he would need a very good reason to override a senior medical officer and, morally, it seemed unfair to load Friday with unnecessary worry about his wife after the ordeal he had been through. Basically, he didn't have a lot of choice.

'OK, let him go,' he snapped finally. 'But two armed guards, full surveillance – understood?'

'Yes sir.' Radcliffe hurried off to deliver the judgement.

★ ★ ★

The lab had taken on the appearance of a major research facility, lined wall to wall with an impressive array of sophisticated medical equipment and an equally impressive complement of personnel. Drake counted no less than seven white-coated technicians, along with three senior medical staff and a couple of assistants.

'Quite a set-up,' he murmured to Reece.

Reece grunted. 'God knows we need 'em. I'm running out of time to find out what we're dealing with here.' He led the way over to one of the medics, bent studiously over a high-powered microscope. A rack of slides containing the yellow slime retrieved from the first nD incursion dominated his workbench.

'Anything?' Reece asked.

Flight Lieutenant Stewart looked up from the microscope. His eyes looked tired, strained. He frowned wearily. 'It's organic matter all right – but we're still a million miles away from finding what kind of a living creature it came from.'

Reece accepted the news stoically. In his heart of hearts, he hadn't really been expecting much better. 'Keep on it,' he muttered, without much enthusiasm.

He turned back to Drake, regarding him silently and thoughtfully for a while, apparently trying to come to some sort of a decision.

Finally, he came to it. 'Drake, you'd better get back to Dr Tucker,' he said quietly. 'And tell her she's clear to resume her work as soon as she feels up to it.'

It was good news for Amanda, although Drake wasn't too happy about his continuing role as nursemaid. He nodded dutifully. 'Yes, General. You still want me to keep an eye on her, sir?'

Reece was thoughtful again. 'Maybe better,' he mused, almost to himself. He stared at Drake piercingly. 'Your special interest is in flight and nav systems, isn't it?'

The man had obviously been checking his service record, Drake realised. He nodded. 'Yes, sir.'

'Then I'd like you and Dr Tucker to take a closer look at the inside of that escape pod,' Reece went on. 'Maybe we can find out something more from that.'

Drake's eyes glowed. 'Yes, sir,' he said, a trifle over-eagerly. This time, he found it impossible to conceal his enthusiasm.

That evening, as if acting upon some unseen and unheard cue, Miles and Burton suddenly awoke from sleep and propped themselves bolt upright in their adjoining beds. They sat, immobile for nearly two full minutes, allowing their eyes to become accustomed to the gloom. Then, independently, and without communication, they both threw back the bedclothes and swung their legs over the edge of their beds, rising to their feet. They began to put their clothes on with a mechanical, zombie-like precision.

Finally dressed, they lurched like a pair of sleepwalkers towards the door.

Outside in the corridor, Sergeant Tuffley had drawn night-guard duties. To say that he was dozing on his feet would be to do him an injustice, but he was somewhat less than fully alert. The sudden and unexpected appearance of the two airmen caught him unawares, making him jump.

'Christ,' he complained bitterly. 'I thought you two were a couple of ghosts.'

Neither Miles nor Burton gave any sign that they had heard him – or, indeed, that they were even aware of his presence. Turning away from him, they began to walk calmly up the corridor towards the exit.

Tuffley called after them. 'Oi, where do you think you're going?'

There was no response. Tuffley tried a direct challenge. 'Halt at once. You are in breach of security.'

The two airmen continued walking, oblivious to the command.

There was something bizarre, even eerie about their behaviour, Tuffley thought uncomfortably. He felt a distinct prickling sensation in the hairs on the back of his neck. He shouted down the corridor to whoever was on duty in the adjoining wing.

'I need some back-up here – on the double.'

Radcliffe and McKay were around the corner in seconds, running up the corridor towards him.

Tuffley pointed after the two airmen, who had almost reached the far end of the corridor.

'They won't respond, sir. It's like they've both freaked out,' he explained to Radcliffe.

Radcliffe gave him an exasperated look. 'Well you'd better get after them, hadn't you? He jabbed Tuffley savagely in the ribs, spurring him into movement. The three of them took off at a run after the two airmen. Tuffley caught up with Burton as the pair of them reached the swing doors at the end of the corridor. He grasped the man by the shoulder, spinning him round.

'For God's sake man, what's the matter . . . ?'

The words died in Tuffley's throat as Burton pivoted to meet him, face to face. The airman's eyes were blank, glazed, unseeing. There was not a trace of emotion, even of sentience, in his features. It was the face of a dead man – a dead man walking – and it chilled Tuffley to the bone.

Temporarily paralysed with shock, Tuffley was hardly aware that Burton was reaching towards the gun holster at his hip, unclipping it with a deft flick of his thumb and starting to draw the weapon clear.

Immediately behind him, Radcliffe could see the danger, and acted. He threw himself forward, knocking both men to the ground, clamping his hand like a vice around Burton's wrist and pinning his arm to the floor.

The man fought like one possessed. It took the

additional weight of McKay to hold him down and a karate chop across the back of the neck from Radcliffe to finally subdue him.

The three airmen climbed to their feet, exchanging baffled looks. In the confusion, Miles had been temporarily forgotten. Loud shouting from outside the administration building brought them abruptly back to reality.

'Miles,' Radcliffe muttered. 'He must be outside already.'

He ran for the exit, closely followed by Tuffley, leaving McKay to watch over the inert form of Burton.

One of the guards on duty immediately outside the main door was still clambering to his feet as Radcliffe ran out.

'It's Airman Miles, sir. He just went berserk and attacked us.'

Radcliffe nodded. 'Yes, I know.' He looked across the parade ground towards the perimeter gates. Finding them locked, Miles had started climbing the fence.

Radcliffe shouted. 'Miles, stop where you are. Stop NOW!'

Miles showed no sign that he had heard. He carried on scaling the wire, now almost at the top.

Radcliffe called again. 'For God's sake, Miles. I don't want to have to shoot. Stop man, while you've still got a chance.'

There was a tight lump in Radcliffe's throat as he watched the young airman continue to climb.

His orders were clear. The base was effectively on full security alert. No one left, or came in, without express clearance from Major General Reece.

'Stop, Miles! Stop or I'll shoot you!'

Miles had one leg over the top of the fence now. If he chose to jump, he could be away and into the darkness in a matter of seconds. The choice between duty and loyalty to a service comrade tore at Radcliffe's guts.

In the end, of course, there was no choice at all. Radcliffe brought his rifle up to his shoulder, squinting down the night-sight. He pulled the trigger once and Miles fell backward, landing awkwardly on his head.

Radcliffe knew he was dead. If the bullet hadn't killed him, then the fall had almost certainly broken his neck. He lowered his rifle, feeling sick inside.

'Christ,' he spat out, loud enough for everyone within twenty yards to hear.

Amanda looked up from the computer screen as Drake entered her quarters, bearing two cups of coffee.

'I thought I heard a shot,' she said. 'What's going on?'

Drake nodded sombrely. 'Miles and Burton. They both just freaked out and tried to break out. Radcliffe had to shoot Miles. Sergeant Tuffley says they were both acting like a pair of zombies.'

Amanda blanched. A shudder ran through her

body as she recalled Woodward's terrified words, shortly before he died: 'They're putting things inside our heads.'

Her reaction was not lost on Drake. He recalled his earlier misgivings. The expression on his face hardened from doubt into accusation. 'You know something, don't you?'

Amanda was too rattled to attempt a denial.

Studying her eyes, Drake found confirmation. 'You lied to General Reece – you lied to me.'

He slammed the two cups of coffee down on the nearest surface, stepping over to Amanda and grasping her roughly by he shoulders. He shook her as one might shake a misbehaving child.

'The truth, Amanda. I want the truth. How much do you know?'

Amanda shook herself free, backing away from him. 'Please, Chris, you know how important this work is to me. If I'd told Reece the truth he'd have declared me unfit for duty. I have to be a part of this.'

Drake wasn't really listening. Nothing was really getting past the sense of anger and hurt. Anger because she had lied to him, and hurt because she hadn't trusted him enough to make him her confidant.

'Dammit, Amanda – you think you're the only important one in all this? The Echoes took Terrell. The nDs took you, Friday and the others. Woodward's gone and now Miles is dead. All the rest of us are just caught in the middle – pawns in a war which we don't understand and don't know the first thing about.'

The appeal seemed to get through. Amanda looked chastened, almost guilty. She stared down towards the floor, as if ashamed to meet him eye to eye.

'All right, Chris, I'll tell you,' she said quietly. 'But don't let the others stop me from working, I couldn't bear it.' She paused briefly. 'You of all people should know what that feels like.'

A thin, wry grin flickered across Drake's lips. A perfectly placed body blow, he thought, without rancour. 'Yes, I do,' he agreed softly.

Flight Lieutenant Stewart brought the four skull CT scans of Amanda, Burton, Miles and Friday up on the computer monitor.

'Right, so tell me again – what exactly is it we're supposed to be looking for?'

'Brain implants of some kind,' Drake told him. 'Any evidence of some form of tampering?'

Stewart frowned dubiously. He glanced at Reece, as if expecting confirmation that Drake was a harmless lunatic. Instead, he got a curt nod.

'Do it,' he muttered. 'Let's find out if we're getting anywhere close to the truth *this* time.'

The slightly bitter dig referred to Amanda, but Drake couldn't help feeling that it reflected on him. Wisely, he said nothing.

Stewart returned his attention to the monitor, bringing Amanda's scan up in close-up and studying it for several moments. 'Absolutely clear,' he announced finally, firmly, as though he never doubted it for a second.

'What about the others?' Reece asked.

Stewart sighed, making it perfectly clear he considered the whole procedure a complete waste of time. He ran through the remaining three scans quickly and dismissively. 'As I thought. There's nothing abnormal in any of them,' he announced finally.

Drake bent forward, peering at the monitor screen more closely. There was something which looked like a minor fault-line on Friday's scan. 'What's that?' he demanded.

'A cranial plate,' Stewart said, matter-of-factly.

'So he must have had a fractured skull or something once?'

Stewart shrugged carelessly. 'Yes, but there's nothing particularly significant about that. It's a fairly standard, if not routine, operation these days.'

'Can we bring that plate up any more?' Drake asked.

Stewart nodded. 'We did one high-resolution CT, but there seemed no reason to bother with it.'

'Bring it up,' Reece put in.

Stewart did as he was ordered, punching up a new sequence on the keyboard. The enlarged image filled the screen.

Drake jabbed it with his finger. 'Look, there,' he muttered triumphantly. 'It looks like a fault, but I'm willing to bet it isn't.'

Stewart studied the indicated area more closely. 'There's absolutely no evidence of a foreign body,' he observed after a while.

Drake was quietly thoughtful for a moment. 'Correct me if I'm wrong, but CT scans are really only a more sophisticated form of X-rays, aren't they?' he asked finally.

Stewart nodded. 'Basically, yes.'

'And there are some things that can't be picked up on X-ray? Soft tissue, that sort of thing?'

Stewart regarded Drake as one might regard a simpleton. 'Obviously,' he muttered.

Drake turned back to General Reece. 'Look, Amanda has told us that nD technology appears to be based on organic, living matter, rather than minerals.'

Reece seemed unimpressed. 'Dr Tucker has told us a lot of things,' he said pointedly.

Drake refused to be put down. 'What I'm trying to say is that we might not be seeing what's right under our noses.' He appealed to Stewart. 'That's possible, isn't it?'

Reluctantly, Stewart had to concede. 'Yes, assuming that any foreign body were not made of a radiolucent substance, we wouldn't detect it upon cursory examination.'

Reece was tiring of the whole exchange. He was out of his depth with all this technical stuff, anyway. 'Check it out,' he told Stewart. 'Drake, you wait here and bring the results to me in my office when you get them.'

Grim-faced, Major General Reece glanced up as Drake walked in to his office.

'Well?'

Drake suppressed a minor smile of self-vindication. 'I was right, sir. Miles, Burton and Friday all seem to have implants although, thankfully, Amanda is in the clear.'

Reece scowled. 'Any theories? About their function?'

Drake nodded. 'Yes, sir. Flight Lieutenant Stewart seems to think that their position in the brain suggests they might be intended to activate some programmed behaviour stored deep in the subconscious.' He paused. 'I guess that's why the nDs returned them to us. But what for? What have they been told to do?'

Reece grunted heavily. 'We're finding that out, fast.' He gestured to the telephone on his desk. 'I just had a call. Wing Commander Friday followed the pattern of aberrant behaviour. He attacked the two guards escorting him, killing one, critically wounding the other.'

Drake whistled through his teeth. 'Is he in custody?'

Reece's answer was a gloomy shake of the head. 'No, he took off. Now he's out there somewhere on the loose, he's armed and dangerous and we don't know where he is, where he's headed or what he's been programmed to do. They were all taken by the nDs and all sent back for a purpose.'

'Amanda's different,' Drake insisted.

'No,' said the General. 'We can't be sure of that. Maybe only her purpose is different. She's held out on us once already and we don't know what else is in store. I'm sorry, Drake.'

He broke off to reach for the phone. 'I'm calling in a neurological specialist,' he announced. 'We're going to get that thing out of Airman Burton's head and we're going to get some goddamned answers.'

CHAPTER NINE

Next morning, Group Captain Susan Preston arrived dead on time, brusque and efficient. Reece wondered if she was the sort of person who would enjoy poking about in people's brains. However, she came highly recommended as the top medical officer in her particular field, along with a sheaf of other qualifications.

He stood beside her in the pre-ops room, studying the sedated form of Burton, whose head had already been shaved in preparation for surgery.

Preston examined the man's naked head in detail.

'You say you have evidence of some kind of brain implant – yet there is no sign of any recent surgery having been carried out on this man,' she stated baldly.

The statement also implied questions. Reece tried to fend them off as best he could. Better that she knew as little as possible at this point, he figured.

'We have reason to believe that those responsible

are using sophisticated and quite revolutionary techniques,' he said.

It seemed to suffice – at least for the time being.

'Well, I suppose we'd better get him in and take the lid off,' Preston said enthusiastically. She could have been talking about opening a tin of baked beans. 'As long as you scrub up, you can watch if you like,' she added to Reece, generously.

He demurred, with a faint, rather sickly grin. 'Think I'll take a raincheck on that. I'll just keep an eye on things through the observation window.'

'As you please.' Preston gripped Burton's trolley and prepared to wheel him through the swing doors into the operating theatre. Reece retired outside to the corridor only to confront Amanda and Drake.

'What are they doing?' Amanda wanted to know.

Reece glowered at her. In his mind, she was responsible for at least two deaths already. He still distrusted her.

'Something we should have done two days ago – if we'd known about it,' he snapped. 'We'll get that device out of Burton's head and then you're scheduled for a complete and thorough medical examination.'

The rebuke had been plain, and sharp. Smarting under it, Amanda didn't have the will to argue, so Drake spoke on her behalf.

'Sir, that's just wasting time, taking Amanda

away from her work. We know she hasn't got an implant. She's seen the nDs at work and she's the only one who can make the slightest sense of it. We need her.'

'No, the General's right,' sighed Amanda. 'I'm a danger to you all. Wing Commander Friday's become a murderer. Who knows what's going to happen to me?'

Her level-headed acceptance of the situation took Reece by surprise.

'I'll stick with her,' offered Drake. 'I'll watch her. No one will be at risk but me. Come on, General – you know we need her.'

That was a point Reece couldn't argue with. He backed off, but only marginally. 'She keeps working – but we make those tests.' He turned to Amanda directly. 'The neurosurgeon looking at Burton. She'll see you too. After what happened with the others, I can't take any chances.'

Reece paused. 'I read your report on nD technology, by the way. It's bizarre, but it makes a crazy kind of logic.'

Whether or not this was supposed to be a compliment, Amanda wasn't sure. 'It's just so radically different to ours,' she pointed out. 'Everything appears to be based entirely on biological forms – the manipulation of living tissues. And now we know that they're not averse to adapting or modifying other species to suit their purpose.'

'That's why we're both convinced that the escape pod is not nD,' Drake put in. 'It has to belong to the Echoes, Terrell's people. The technology is far more advanced than ours, but many of the fundamentals are the same. Metal, electronics, mechanical propulsion systems. Given time, I think we might even crack a few of its secrets.'

It was encouraging news, but Reece couldn't get too enthusiastic. 'Time might well be the one little luxury we're running short of,' he observed, moodily.

Inside the operating theatre, Preston had removed a three-inch square section of Burton's skull and had begun delicately probing the soft tissue of his brain with a pair of forceps. She kept up a running commentary as she worked, both for the benefit of the medical team assisting her and for HQ.

'On first inspection, no evidence of a foreign body in the parietal lobe. Moving on now. Who'd have thought there'd be so many places to hide in a squaddie's brain.'

'Sounds like a stand-up comic,' Drake observed laconically.

Amanda just shivered, wondering exactly what her scheduled 'thorough medical examination' was going to entail.

'Do you think Terrell knows what these nDs have planned for us?' she enquired generally, trying to take her mind off the subject.

'We're still not even sure he is who he says he is,' Reece grunted. 'So I don't think we can count on him for any hard information.'

Over the speaker, Preston's voice droned on.

'Still no evidence of recent surgery. Getting into dangerous territory here.'

There was a momentary pause, then the sound of breath being sucked in.

'Wait, there *is* something here. A miniscule foreign body, embedded in the white tissue. Less than one millimetre across, organic in appearance. Am going to attempt surgical excision.'

It was tricky, by any surgeon's standards. Preston stepped back from the patient, fiddling with the microscope eyepiece over her right eye, adjusting it to precise focus. She transferred the surgical forceps to her other hand for a moment, stretching and flexing the fingers of her right hand in preparation for the delicate work which would be required of them. Only when she was completely ready did she close in again, probing gently into Burton's brain tissues with intricate precision.

The tip of the forceps brushed the tiny organic nodule, hardly making contact. Yet it appeared to move slightly, Preston thought, momentarily surprised. Almost a flinching reaction, as though it had a life of its own – a living creature, reacting to an outside stimulus.

It was a crazy thought. She had probably imagined it. Using the extreme tips of the forceps, Preston started to scrape it free of the tissue in which it was embedded.

The implant began to glow – first orange and

then a searing white. Surrounding brain tissue shrivelled, melting away like the crater of a volcano. There was a sickly, acrid stench of charred flesh.

Preston was astonished. She could only watch on in horror as the tiny implant disappeared, leaving behind an area of devastation out of all proportion to its size. At the head of the operating table, the ECG monitor flatlined, its pinging notes replaced by a continuous, thin monotone.

Group Captain Preston backed away from the operating table, clearly shaken. She'd never seen anything like it before. Anger, frustration and confusion battled for supremacy in her mind. To lose any patient on the table was a professional as well as a personal tragedy. To encounter a phenomenon so utterly outside the realm of her experience was a psychological shock. And running through all these emotions was the strange, completely irrational notion that she had been made the butt of some particularly sick and vicious practical joke.

She peeled off her surgical gloves, throwing them into the disposal bin. Casting Reece a baffled, entreating glance through the observation window, she retreated to the pre-ops room.

Preston seemed to have regained her professional detachment, if not her composure, by the time Reece, Drake and Amanda came in to join her.

'The cerebral implant appeared to self-destruct, causing non-survivable injury,' she announced, in the same emotionless tone she had used for the recording equipment.

'Some form of anti-tampering device?' Reece suggested.

'I have no idea. I can't account for what happened,' Preston answered candidly.

Drake had his own theory. 'It was the nDs.'

'They pulled it back into their space – created a mini-portal,' Amanda added.

Preston regarded them both suspiciously. Quite clearly, they were referring to some information she had not been made privy to. Something, perhaps, which might have had an outcome on the operation she had just performed. She turned an accusing gaze on Major General Reece.

Reece tried to take the heat off for a moment by effecting some convenient introductions.

'Group Captain Preston, Flight Lieutenant Drake and Dr Tucker.'

Preston wasn't to be put off.

'General, I was called in personally to deal with a highly irregular case, and it's becoming increasingly clear to me that there is far more to this than was contained in my original brief. Might I be permitted to know exactly what is going on here?'

Reece shifted his feet uncomfortably. The crunch point had arrived sooner than he would have wished.

'I'll fill you in later,' he promised. 'All of us have been up too close and too involved with this thing. Right now, I think it's important that we get a completely detached and fresh perspective. So, in your opinion, what is the purpose of these implants?'

Preston seemed to understand the logic behind Reece's thinking. She nodded thoughtfully. 'Point taken, General. All right, if you want an opinion – and I stress *opinion* – their position in the cerebral tissue might indicate a linkage between the subconscious and the motor areas of the brain. Behavioural control, in other words.'

Reece was pushing her hard now. 'But within the bounds of existing surgical procedures?'

Preston shook her head. 'Certainly none that I know of. I can't think of any institution which would be capable of such highly sophisticated techniques. Furthermore, I seriously doubt that we even have the capability to safely neutralise them. If we find others, it may well be that our only attainable option is euthanasia.'

Reece sighed deeply. He had his answer now. If there had been any remaining, vestigal doubts, they were finally gone.

'Thank you, Group Captain. That will be all for now,' he said quietly. 'Like I said, I'll give you a full update later.'

Preston accepted her dismissal with a brief, quiescent nod. She glanced at Amanda on her way to the door.

'Dr Tucker, I believe you're due to report to me for a full medical examination. I'll see you now.'

Amanda shivered. In view of the woman's

previous statement, it was a terrifying prospect. She followed Preston down the corridor.

Actually, the medical examination hadn't been too bad.

'So, what's the verdict?' Amanda asked, trying to sound a lot brighter than she felt.

'Your physical examination was unremarkable. Your blood tests and scans reveal no apparent abnormalities. You would appear to be in good health.'

Preston delivered the information with cool, professional detachment, giving away no more than was dictated by the requirements of her job.

'So I haven't got an implant?' Amanda pressed.

The answer wasn't quite as positive as she'd hoped for.

'I can find no direct evidence of one.'

'So you'll recommend to General Reece that I return to my work?'

Preston shrugged. 'If that's what you want.'

'It's what I *need*,' Amanda said, with quiet emphasis.

The two women exchanged a fleeting, mutually understanding glance. It was not friendship, although under other circumstances Amanda might well have admired Susan Preston for her efficient, single-minded devotion to her work. But it was the one thing they had in common, the single and flimsy suspension bridge across the chasm which separated them. A chasm Amanda herself had created – not out of antagonism but out of fear.

Amanda reached for her clothes. 'Can I go now?' she asked.

Preston hesitated, then reached for Amanda's arm, examining the still livid wound in the flesh.

nD.

'This lesion on your arm – it's not healing. No evidence of scar tissue.'

It appeared to be a casual observation, but Amanda's heart skipped a beat. She had wondered about that herself.

'And you find that worrying?' she asked, trying to keep the full depth of her concern out of her tone.

Preston made a vague gesture with her shoulders. 'It's not unusual. Maybe you're just a slow healer.' She paused for a moment. 'I understand you inflicted the wound upon yourself. Is that correct?'

Amanda merely nodded.

A slightly perplexed frown furrowed Preston's brow. 'Why would you do such a thing?'

'If they killed me, it was my chance to still get a message out,' Amanda told her.

' "They?" ' Preston picked up on the single word. 'Why don't you tell me your story, Dr Tucker.'

Amanda bristled, without understanding the reason why.

'Read it. It's all on file.'

Preston smiled faintly. 'I have read it. I'd just like to hear it from you.'

Amanda pondered the implications of a direct refusal. They were unclear, but she suspected that Preston might well mark her down as unco-operative on her report to General Reece. He already mistrusted her for her earlier attempt to deceive him. Perhaps this time, it was easier and safer to tell the plain, unvarnished truth. She launched into a full and detailed account of her abduction and subsequent ordeal at the hands of the nDs.

When she had finished, Preston gave no sign that she either believed or disbelieved. She merely jotted down notes on a pad, nodding to herself as she wrote.

'Would you be prepared to submit to a psychiatric examination?' she asked, finally.

It wasn't a question Amanda had been expecting, but she took it on the rise.

'If it will allow me back to work, yes.'

Preston's eyes narrowed slightly. 'It's important to you, isn't it? To prove your theories?'

It was a mistake. Preston had failed to allow for the nature of her patient. Amanda fended off the loaded question with ease.

'It's important to me that I get at the truth.'

Too late, Preston realised her miscalculation. She smiled wryly. 'I think you can get dressed now, Dr Tucker.'

'I'm free to return to work?'

Preston nodded. 'Conditional upon regular

medical examinations, yes. Apart from the wound, nothing else seems to be abnormal. Perhaps you're the lucky one, Dr Tucker.'

She said no more as Amanda dressed hurriedly and left.

Susan Preston waited for a few moments before gathering up her notes and heading in the direction of Major General Reece's office.

Reece had fulfilled his promise to bring Preston fully up to date. Now they were touring the scientific laboratories, in which she was showing a keen interest.

'So who else is working on this project?' she wanted to know.

'There's this installation, with the staff I've put together here. That's it. Nobody else knows.' Reece hesitated for a second. 'Except you, now, of course,' he added. 'But I was hoping we could still keep it in-house for a while longer.'

Preston took a moment to read between the lines. 'You're asking me to stay on, become a part of the team?'

Reece nodded. 'We could use you. And I think you'd find some pretty challenging work to keep you interested.'

He stopped beside Flight Lieutenant Stewart, hunched, as ever, over a microscope. Reece picked up a small specimen jar containing the yellow nD slime from the lab bench. 'Like this, for instance. We opened fire when they took our people. Deposits like this were left behind when they'd gone.'

Preston looked openly sceptical. 'You're not trying to tell me this is their blood?'

Stewart looked up from his work. 'With respect, ma'am – every analytical test we've conducted so far leads us to that inescapable conclusion.'

He moved away from the microscope. 'Perhaps you'd like to take a look for yourself, ma'am.'

It was a challenge Preston found impossible to resist. She bent over the microscope, studying the loaded slide. She looked up again quickly, with an almost instinctive reaction of shock. 'What kind of an animal is this?'

Stewart shook his head slowly from side to side. 'It isn't an animal,' he muttered firmly.

Preston returned her eye to the microscope. This time, she remained glued to it for several minutes. When she finally looked up again, she looked stunned. She glanced at Reece, temporarily speechless.

He managed a pale imitation of a grin. 'You can say whatever you want to say, Group Captain. This isn't a religion – I tolerate heretics.'

Preston found her voice – albeit slightly shaky. 'General, what we have here is nothing known to exist on Earth.'

Reece's face was emotionless, but a faint flicker of light glowed momentarily in his eyes, as if the last shadow of doubt had suddenly been peeled away like a pair of curtains.

Preston turned her attention to Stewart. 'Do we have other samples?'

'Yes, ma'am. Different specimens, collected at

different locations – but they're all exactly the same.'

'The same?' Preston frowned.

'Identical, ma'am.' Stewart reached for a tray of slides, passing them to her.

Preston loaded five of the slides in turn, studying each for a long time. The whole process took nearly half an hour. Reece watched and waited for her reaction.

When she was finally through, she straightened up slowly and took a long, deep breath, exhaling it through her teeth. She spent a few more moments gathering her thoughts, choosing her words.

'Flight Lieutenant Stewart is right,' she concluded eventually. 'In every one of these samples, the cellular structure is absolutely identical in every respect.'

Reece looked completely out of his depth. 'And what does that mean, exactly?'

'Clones,' Stewart broke in, answering for her. He had been rapidly approaching the same conclusion himself, but was grateful for the second opinion.

Preston didn't appear to mind having the wind knocked out of her sails. She nodded curtly. 'Again, you're correct.'

She turned back to Reece. 'What this means, General, is that these nDs, as you choose to call them, are all cloned, probably from a single genetic source. They have obviously already mastered and put into practice gene-splicing techniques that we are still debating in terms of morality.'

It took Reece a few moments to fully appreciate the terrifying implications. 'You mean they can reproduce themselves at will?' he suggested. 'Create additional versions of themselves at any time, in any numbers they choose or need?'

Preston nodded. 'Not only that, General. It means that they all act the same, think the same. No individuals. It's also more than possible that they even share a hive intelligence, a form of telepathy. Any group of nDs, no matter what their number, is effectively a single unit, with a single purpose.'

Reece looked totally devastated. His craggy features bore the expression of a boxer who'd been knocked to the canvas for the sixth time in the first round and was asking himself the question: Was it worth climbing to his feet again?

'How do you even begin to fight an army like that?' he muttered hopelessly. It wasn't really a question. 'They can mass-produce soldiers like we mass-produce nuts and bolts. Every one comes fully trained, indoctrinated with the same purpose, totally dedicated to blind, unquestioning obedience to the cause.' He broke off to stare pleadingly at Preston. 'You make them sound invincible.'

Preston shook her head. 'You're overlooking one thing, General. This single genetic identity also makes them vulnerable. What you perceive as their strength may in fact be their greatest weakness.'

It was a thin straw of hope, still too tenuous to be grasped. Reece's eyes narrowed dubiously. 'How so?'

'What will kill one will kill them all,' Group Captain Preston said emphatically.

Drake settled himself into the sculpted contours of the escape pod's pilot seat, scanning the bewildering array of unfamiliar instruments with their strange, alien calibrations. They might as well be Egyptian hieroglyphs for all they meant to him.

'I just wish I knew where to start,' he complained to Amanda, standing over him. 'There's not one single instrument here that bears any relationship to what I'm familiar with.'

Amanda patted him on the shoulder reassuringly. 'Think laterally,' she urged. 'Think like a pilot – any pilot. What would you need to know? Where would that information be best displayed?'

Drake grinned ruefully. 'Yeah,' he muttered, nodding his head. As ever, Amanda had demonstrated her uncanny knack for slicing through veils of confusion, exposing the obvious.

He ran through a mental checklist, speaking aloud. 'This is an escape pod, not the mother ship,' he reasoned. 'So there'd be no need for fuel, power levels or astral navigation instruments.'

'But you'd want communications,' Amanda put in. 'Some way to contact your base, give your position. Perhaps even transmit a distress signal.'

'So I'd need my spatial coordinates,' Drake said, following that train of thought along. 'And I'd need them to be somewhere I could read them off fast, easily, while I'm coping with a crash landing.'

He broke off, reaching out to the right-hand side of the central control panel, tapping one of the dials. 'Now if I was designing a craft from scratch, I might well put it about here.'

'Good, we're getting somewhere,' Amanda said. 'Now, what else?'

Drake's confidence was increasing by the second. 'Well, if I was coming in for a manual landing, the one thing I'd most definitely need is an artificial horizon. And that would be smack in front of me.'

He reviewed the cluster of five instruments in the dead centre of the main array. 'That one,' he said confidently, indicating a panel which consisted of two crescent shapes, one mounted above the other. 'And these two are probably airspeed and relative groundspeed,' he added, pointing to another pair of gauges.

Drake fingered a couple of recessed switches tentatively. 'Of course, what we really need to do is power this thing up and put a few of these theories to the test,' he pointed out.

Amanda nodded. 'Way ahead of you. I've already had the ground technicians link us up to a portable generator. We can only afford a trickle of power – no more than twenty or thirty amps at most. We have no idea what this thing's normal capacity is. Surge the system, and we could blow everything.'

Drake considered for a while. A rogueish grin began to spread across his face. 'Well, what do you think? Do we give it a go?'

Amanda smiled back at him. 'I'm just the scientist. You're the pilot.'

Drake nodded. 'Yes I am, aren't I?'

Impulsively, he reached out and punched three of the switches in sequence.

For a few seconds, nothing happened. Then there was the faintest hum of power and some half-dozen of the myriad control panels glowed dully. Above Drake and Amanda's eyeline, a small screen also lit up momentarily, displaying a curious symbol, like two teardrops lying side by side. It had faded again before either of them had a chance to notice.

Drake regarded the meagre display of activity with disappointment. He had been hoping for more.

'Dammit, we're only getting a fraction of this pod's capability here. Nine tenths of it's still dead.'

Amanda was more of a realist. 'We're dealing with a hunk of alien hardware that hit the ground at a hundred miles an hour. Just what the hell did you expect?'

Drake punched at the switches again in frustration. The system shut itself down. 'We need

Terrell,' he said. 'He's the only one who can help us make any sense of this thing. I know he's got the answers. I know it.'

Amanda looked dubious. 'You really think you can persuade him to talk at last?'

Drake gave her a strange, lopsided grin. 'Not me – you,' he said. 'I've watched you at work. You're good.'

They found Terrell almost fully recovered. His hospital bed had been replaced by a reclining lounger, on which he sat reading W. A. Parmenter's *Towards the Millennium*. He looked up from the bulky volume as Drake and Amanda entered the room.

'Light reading?' Amanda enquired, conversationally.

Terrell gave her a thin, wan smile. 'Just catching up on Earth history.' He put the book down slowly. 'You've come so far, so fast, in the past fifty years. It's almost as if you don't yet realise just how far you still have left to go.'

Drake was neither an historian nor a philosopher. He came straight to the point.

'Charles, we've come to appeal to you for your help. There are things happening here that we don't understand.'

The distant smile on Terrell's face changed subtly. It was almost pitying now. 'And you think that understanding is going to help you?'

Amanda took over. 'It's a starting point. All we need is a little guidance.'

'Ah, guidance.' Terrell breathed the words thoughtfully. 'I seem to recall you've had guides before. You tend to crucify them.'

Drake was tiring of the mind games already. 'Just give us a straight answer, Terrell. We're having trouble making sense of your vehicle's control systems. Will you help?'

Terrell's expression hardened. 'It wouldn't be helping. It would only be putting you all in greater danger than you face already.'

'Can't we be the judge of that?' Drake snapped testily. 'Now I've already managed to activate some of the pod's display functions, but I need to know what I'm doing.'

Terrell sucked in a breath. 'You've done *what*?'

'I've activated some of the pod's display functions . . .' Drake started to repeat, then broke off abruptly as he saw the sudden expression of alarm on Terrell's face. 'That worries you, doesn't it? Why?'

Terrell shook his head agitatedly, clearly flustered. 'I can't say,' he stammered.

They seemed to have caught the man on the run just for once, Amanda thought. She pressed home the advantage.

'This danger you say we're in . . . you know what it is and yet you don't feel free to tell us. And that troubles you, Charles, doesn't it? It troubles you deeply. It shakes the very core of who you are, what you are.'

Amanda seemed to have hit the target with unerring precision. Terrell had begun to tremble violently, rocked by some deep inner turmoil. Anguish pulled at the very muscles of his face, contorting it into a mask of grief.

'Please, leave me alone,' he begged. 'There's nothing I can do, or say.'

It was not the time to let him off the hook.

'The nDs took five of our people.' Drake shouted at him. 'Three of them are dead and one of them is a murderer running amok in the countryside. What is his purpose, Terrell?'

The outburst seemed to calm Terrell, or at least enable him to collect his thoughts. 'I honestly wouldn't know,' he said flatly, sincerely.

It wasn't enough for Amanda. 'What do the nDs use people for, Charles?' she asked, more gently. 'I need to know.'

Terrell read between the lines. 'They took you, too?' he asked, evidently surprised. He stared at Amanda with a new fascination, his eyes widening.

Amanda found his gaze chilling. It was as if, suddenly, she had become the enemy. Her face paled. Drake felt her fear like an empathic wave.

'She's clear,' he put in. 'The doctors say she doesn't have an implant.'

The look of anguish returned to Terrell's face. 'But they took her,' he stated bleakly. 'Had they no plan for her beforehand, then they would have devised one.'

He looked at Amanda again.

'I'm sorry, Dr Tucker, but I really have no idea of what they might have planned for you.'

CHAPTER TEN

The limited success with the escape pod seemed worth reporting to Major General Reece. Drake sought him out, eventually tracking him down at the HQ observation post, facing out over the surrounding landscape towards the sea.

Reece seemed in a particularly reflective mood. He acknowledged Drake with a curt nod, then continued his silent vigil over the peaceful Scottish countryside. When he finally spoke his voice was distant, detached.

'A thousand years ago, the Vikings landed on this coast,' he murmured quietly. 'What threat are we facing now, I wonder.'

It didn't seem like the time to speak. Drake remained silent, sharing Reece's view and sombre mood.

Reece eventually turned to face him. 'You know, I was wrong about you, Drake,' he said unexpectedly. 'You're a good man to have around.'

Drake gave a brief, deferential nod. 'Thank you, sir.'

His respect for the man increased a hundred-fold immediately. It took a lot for someone with Reece's degree of authority to admit their mistakes to a subordinate.

He wondered if it was an opportune moment to make his report. He opened his mouth to speak, but never got the chance.

There was a sudden, blinding flash which lit up the whole sky. The morning, grey and sullen, was momentarily transformed into the high noon of the most brilliantly sunny day.

'What the hell was that?' Reece asked, startled.

'Lightning?' Drake suggested, weakly.

They both waited for the sound of accompanying thunder, but it never came.

Reece was back to his normal self in a moment. 'We'd better get back inside,' he snapped urgently. He broke into a loping run, heading for the main administration block with Drake hard on his heels.

All the main lighting in the corridors was out. The auxiliary power system was trying to kick in, but with little success. Emergency lights flickered on and off again like malfunctioning stroboscopes. Guards and military police swarmed everywhere, their weapons already drawn, half-expecting an attack.

Reece and Drake finally made it to the central operations room to find it in chaos.

Some systems were down, others functioning erratically. The room itself, windowless, was almost pitch-black. Technicians and airmen scurried about in the dark, bumping into each other, desperately trying to fulfil their set functions. A sense of panic overrode everything.

'Everybody hold,' Reece thundered. 'Stow your weapons. Somebody get that power back on.'

Radcliffe appeared out of the gloom.

'Sorry sir, but it took us by surprise,' he blurted out. 'There was this massive power surge, then everything went haywire. We thought the nDs were coming again.'

The emergency power system finally kicked in. The dull illumination of fire escape lights filled the room. Several of the computer screens, which had been blank, began to glow again, although their operators still seemed disoriented.

Amanda took operational control, barking out orders as though she'd been born to it.

'Check out our satellite surveillance monitors. Look out for communications traffic on all frequencies. If you pick anything up, isolate the bandwidth and patch it through to me.'

Her air of authority seemed to galvanise everyone into action. A state of near-normality slowly returned. The main lights came back on.

Amanda noticed Reece and Drake for the first time. She approached sheepishly.

'Sorry, General, but I thought it important to get everyone back to their jobs.'

Reece brushed the unnecessary apology aside. 'You did good,' he told her. 'Thank you. Now, do we have any idea what just happened?'

Amanda shook her head. 'Not at the moment,

General, but I'm working on it.'

Reece turned to Drake. 'Your original story –
when you shot Terrell down. You told me then
your aircraft was hit by some sort of power surge
which knocked out your instrumentation. Anything like this?'

Drake thought about it. 'Maybe,' he conceded.
'But nothing like on this scale.'

Amanda had returned to her computer. 'General – I'm getting something,' she called out.

Reece and Drake rushed over to her side.

'Satellite surveillance pinpoints a huge energy
release, approximately 1.5 billion kilometres out
from Earth. Our readings show a massive
electro-magnetic pulse, accompanying intense
radiation output.'

Reece caught his breath. 'Shockwave?' he
asked, urgently.

Amanda shook her head. 'Unlikely. Over that
distance, virtually all its force will have dissi-
pated long before it reaches us.'

Reece let out a sigh of relief. 'Then what the
hell was it if it wasn't some kind of weapon?'

Knox called over from radar surveillance.
'There's something else, sir. We have a contact –
incoming.'

'Where?' Reece barked.

'Upper atmosphere, but it's coming in fast.'

Drake ran over to check the readings.

'Fast is right. At that speed, it must be on
re-entry. Or just plain entry,' he added as an
afterthought.

'Identify and acquire,' Reece snapped. 'Squadron Leader Knox, co-ordinate air defence. Flight Lieutenant Radcliffe, secure this installation.'

He looked over towards Amanda. 'nD?'

'Doesn't look like it, General. Radar-detectable, no recognisable nD behaviour.' Amanda broke off, suddenly struck by a revelation. 'It's Echo, I'm sure of it.'

She jumped to her feet, abandoning the computer.

Reece stared at her in astonishment. 'Dr Tucker, what are you doing?'

Amanda spoke in a rush. 'It's Echo. They knew the nDs were coming here. If anyone can help us, they can.'

Reece could only gape after her blankly as she ran from the room.

Knox pulled him back to reality. 'We're getting a reading now.'

There was a moment of silence before she spoke again, her voice hushed with shock. 'Here. It's headed here. General, we've got to call this in. We have to report this right now and get our interceptors into the air.'

She was probably right, Reece thought. For the briefest possible moment, he was frozen with indecision. Then Amanda was back, dragging Terrell behind her.

'Dr Tucker, just what the hell do you think you're doing?' Reece exploded.

'Trying to prevent a catastrophe.' She pushed Terrell in front of the radar screen. 'What is it,

Charles? Tell us. Tell us *now*.'

Terrell spoke quietly. 'That's the identifying transmission of an Echo landing pod.'

'It's not a radar contact?' Amanda asked, making sure.

Terrell shook his head. 'It's not a normal radar signal at all. It's a deliberate effort to identify itself.'

'And that's what affected all our instruments?' Reece demanded.

'Possibly, yes,' said Terrell, but he didn't seem too sure.

'Why is it coming here?' Amanda wanted to know.

Terrell sighed. 'If you succeeded in reactivating my escape pod, its flight systems will have automatically transmitted a distress message and homing signal. It's coming for me.'

He paused to glance at the radar screen again. Concern showed on his face. 'There's something wrong. It's coming in too fast. It must be damaged.'

Knox checked the readings herself.

'He's right, General,' she confirmed to Reece. 'On his present trajectory and at this speed, the pilot doesn't have a chance.'

'Damn.' Reece cursed loudly. 'All right, Squadron Leader Knox. Let me know as soon as you have the exact coordinates for impact.'

'Coming in now, sir.' Knox read off the coordinates aloud. '55-36-21 north, 01-58-47 west.'

Drake was checking the field map. Suddenly,

he let out a little whoop of exultation. 'Ducks and drakes,' he exclaimed, grinning.

Reece scowled at him. 'Have you lost your mind, Drake?'

Drake was still bubbling. 'Ducks and drakes, sir. Remember, when you were a kid, skimming flat pebbles across the surface of a pond?' He turned to Terrell. 'This landing pod – is it essentially the same design as yours?'

Terrell nodded, uncertainly. 'Yes, but . . .'

'Don't you see, sir, it's a flat-bottomed craft,' Drake said, cutting in. 'Skim across the surface – that's what out Echo pilot is trying to do.'

Reece was still staring at him in total confusion. Drake thrust the field map under his nose, stabbing at it with his finger.

'Those coordinates, General – look, it's a lake. I think our friend is going to try for a soft landing.'

Once again, Drake found himself on board a Chinook involved in a search and rescue, not knowing quite what he was going to find. He tried to steady his thoughts and concentrate on the bearings as the helicopter swooped in low over the edge of the lake, commencing a primary sweep around its western perimeter.

'There,' Drake shouted, pointing out through the open hatchway. 'Over there, about fifty yards from the shore.'

Squadron Leader Knox followed the direction of his finger. The landing pod was a black shape against the dark surface of the water. Slightly upended, it appeared to be sinking.

'Get us over there – fast,' Knox bellowed at the pilot.

The chopper banked into a tight turn, losing height as it dropped towards the lake's placid surface.

'It's going down,' the pilot called back as they approached. 'I can see the pilot. He's in the water.'

Drake jumped to his feet, unclipping his safety harness. He moved to the hatch, steadying himself against the bulkhead.

Knox looked at him in alarm. 'Flight Lieutenant Drake, what do you think you're doing?'

Drake ignored her. Looking down, he could see the helicopter pilot was right. The pod was sinking fast. Its pilot lay motionless in the water, still connected to his craft by his life-support umbilical. When it went down, it would drag him with it.

Urgently, he called up front to the pilot. 'Can you take us in as low as you dare?'

Knox repeated her demand. 'What are you doing, Drake?'

Drake spoke without looking at her. 'No time. Trust me.'

He frantically pulled off his heavy kit and flack jacket, and poised himself as the helicopter dropped to within twenty feet of the lake's surface. Then, taking a deep breath, he jumped out.

He was unprepared for the vicious cold as he

splashed into the icy lake some ten or fifteen yards from the pilot. The rear end of the pod thrust upwards almost vertically in the water now, commencing its final slide into the depths. Even as he started swimming frantically towards it, the last section slipped beneath the surface.

Drake took a hasty last visual bearing on the pilot's position and jack-knifed in the water, kicking himself into a dive.

From inside the helicopter, Knox could only hold her breath and watch anxiously as the pod, its pilot and his would-be rescuer all disappeared beneath the surface.

Nail-biting seconds passed, in which it looked as though the deep lake might forever hide its secrets. Then Drake's head broke the surface again, followed by his upraised hand, clutching the disconnected end of the umbilical.

He kicked himself over on to his back and floated, cradling the helmeted head of the pilot against his belly. Dropping the severed umbilical, he raised his hand again and gave a thumbs-up signal. He splashed out, heading for shore.

Not one to usually give vent to her emotions, Squadron Leader Knox let out a little whoop of triumph. 'He's got him,' she called into the radio. 'He's got him!'

She looked somewhat sheepishly around the interior of the helicopter as the heads of every other occupant turned towards her in surprise. Hastily recovering her normal poise, she shouted out orders above the chattering din of the helicopter's engines.

'Get us down to the shore – now!'

Knox knelt on the shingle, regarding the space-suited, helmeted figure of the pilot with a growing sense of unease. The total body size was wrong, the proportions of the torso and limbs subtly distorted. Her earlier convictions, which she had thought unshakeable, were already plagued by doubts.

The pilot was alive – but only just. His head, appearing grossly oversized in the bulbous helmet, moved sluggishly from side to side. He seemed to be in distress.

'There's water inside his helmet,' Drake shouted numbly, still shaking with cold. 'Get it off him, quickly.'

Sergeant Tuffley knelt over the pilot's prone body, fiddling with the helmet. 'I can't find the release mechanism.'

Knox crouched to help him, identifying a small catch where the helmet joined the neck to the spacesuit and pressing it. The face-plate sprang open, allowing water to gush out and revealing a pair of recessed locking studs built into the suit's rigid collar. Thumbing them together, she twisted the helmet and pulled it free.

Knox let out a single gasp as she stared into the face of an Echo for the first time. The smooth, hairless domed head; the huge, black, elfin-like eyes; the pallid, rubbery skin covered in dark blotches. The creature coughed weakly, water spurting out of its mouth as it struggled to fill its lungs with air.

In that moment, Squadron Leader Knox experienced a conversion every bit as dramatic and life-changing as Saul's on the road to Damascus. She looked up at Drake, speechless with shock. The expression in her eyes spoke volumes.

Still dumb, she stepped back as Drake moved in to look at the alien he'd rescued, noting a seeping, dark patch just behind one of its curiously flat ears. 'It seems to be wounded, but I can't tell how badly,' he said, urgently. 'We'd better radio Group Captain Preston and tell her to get the medical unit set up for full emergency procedures.'

Knox nodded her agreement, finding her voice at last. 'Tuffley, hear what the man said? Do it. I want every man on board – now. Get Drake and the – the . . . *him* up too.' She called up to the helicopter pilot. 'Then get us home – fast.'

She paused to look down at the Echo again. 'And tell General Reece to have Terrell in the medical unit,' she added, as an afterthought. 'He'll know more about this creature's physiology than any of us.'

'There's no pulse. I can't find a pulse,' Flight Lieutenant Stewart shouted, urgently, fingering all around the area where the carotid artery would be on a human patient.

Drake was wrapped in a blanket, standing in a

corner of the med wing, trying to keep out of the way. Amanda Tucker was hovering, trying to be of assistance.

The Echo's eyes were still open, flickering weakly, betraying a faint spark of life. It coughed thinly, expelling another trickle of water from the corner of its mouth.

'It's conscious. There's got to be a pulse,' Preston said with professional conviction. She stroked the Echo's throat with deft, practised fingers, moving up to a spot just underneath the chin. 'Here, there's something here. Get a monitor on it.'

Stewart frantically connected up cardiac and blood-pressure monitors, finally getting a reading. 'Rate of about twenty.'

Amanda looked over at Terrell. 'Help us, Charles, for Christ's sake. It that good or bad?'

Terrell's face was grim. 'Bad.'

'And blood pressure?' Stewart prompted. 'Eighty over unreadable.'

Terrell was flustered and uncertain. 'I think theirs is normally lower than ours, I'm not sure.'

Stewart grunted. 'Well it's sure low now.' He glanced at Preston. 'Should we speed him up?'

Preston was examining the Echo's head. 'Laceration of the temporoparietal area, no apparent clinical fracture, no blood in the ear canal, pupils equal.' She broke off to consider Stewart's question. 'Oxygen?' she suggested, tentatively.

Amanda glanced at Terrell, repeating the question. 'Well, oxygen?'

Terrell nodded distractedly. 'Yes, yes, they're oxygen breathers. But it's no use asking me! I'm not a doctor. I don't know enough about them.'

'Fifteen litres of oxygen per minute,' Preston said, making a unilateral decision. 'And atropine, 600 micrograms.'

Stewart settled an oxygen mask over the Echo's face. He stood back to check the monitor, calling off the readings. 'Airway clear, breathing spontaneously. Maintaining pulse, still brady-cardic at twenty.'

'Get that atropine,' Preston barked at Amanda. 'See if we can't speed him up.'

She continued her clinical examination. 'Loud S1 and S2. Third and fourth sounds. Systolic and diastolic murmurs.'

'I'm in!' cried Stewart as he found a vein. Amanda passed him the syringe and held her breath as he administered the atropine through the cannula in the Echo's arm.

Preston spoke again. 'I want a twelve-lead ECG, X-rays, skull, C-spine, chest, abdomen and pelvis – FBC, U and E, glucose, crossmatch and gases. Contact radiology about an urgent CT.'

Reece had, up to this minute, been keeping deliberately in the background, acutely aware of the emergency and anxious not to get in the way of the medics. Now, hoping that the immediate crisis was over, at least for the time being, he stepped forward.

'What are its chances?' he asked Preston.

She shrugged. 'Who knows? At a guess, I'd say

it was in critical condition.'

Reece turned his attention to Terrell. 'Can you communicate with it?' he demanded.

Terrell looked reluctant. 'Yes, I could.' The last word carried a definite emphasis.

Reece chose to ignore it. 'Then get as much as you can out of it. There might not be much time.'

'It's very weak,' Stewart pointed out.

Terrell didn't move. 'Interrogation might be too much,' he protested stubbornly.

Reece grabbed him by the arm, dragging him over to the Echo's side. 'Just do it,' he hissed.

Just for a moment, Terrell's eyes blazed with defiance. Then, acquiescing, he bent over, pressing his lips close to the Echo's ear. He began to speak, in a strange, sing-song whisper.

The Echo's lips moved. Its voice was weak, croaking. Then suddenly, the monitor trace went wild. Terrell jerked back.

'Rate's picking up!' cried Stewart. 'Forty . . . sixty . . . a hundred . . .'

'What the hell's that now?' said Preston. 'Some kind of tachy?'

'VT?' suggested Stewart.

He looked up at the monitor as it went into a horribly spiky, trace-like fibrillation.

'He's unconscious,' said Preston, feeling under the Echo's chin. 'That pulse has gone!'

'VF? Is that VF?'

'Cardiovert!' shouted Preston.

Stewart moved quickly, charging up the defibrillator. 'Setting? Terrell?'

'I don't know!' cried Terrell, bewildered.

'Start at a hundred joules, unsync'd,' ordered Preston.

'Charging.'

'Clear.'

The Echo's body convulsed as the charge surged through it, but the monitors showed no change.

'Two hundred.'

'Charging.'

'Clear!'

Again, nothing. Preston kept her cool.

'Three hundred.'

'Charging.'

'Clear!'

This time, the monitor trace returned to a pattern. Preston felt under the Echo's chin once more. 'We have a pulse!' A sigh of relief swept through the room.

As consciousness returned to the Echo, its eyes searched for Terrell. He leaned back in to communicate with it as Preston and Stewart continued to plan their course of action.

'We need to get it into an intensive care unit,' Preston told Reece. 'We need complete blood analysis and scans of all its major organs. It's the only way we can attempt to define its physiology and anatomy. Otherwise we won't be able to treat his injuries.'

Reece nodded his head. 'I'll get you everything you need. Drake, organise airborne medevac. Tucker, get a recording of this interrogation. I want this on video tape for the historical record—'

Drake wasn't listening. He was transfixed, watching the interchange between Terrell and the Echo. The alien sounds meant absolutely nothing to him, but they had a terrible, dramatic effect upon Terrell. His face registered first shock, then horror, finally sagging into a mask of the most unimaginable anguish and suffering. In a matter of a few seconds, the man appeared to have aged a dozen years. His eyes glistened with tears. His entire body trembled with emotion.

'What is it? What's it saying?' Drake demanded, but Terrell gave no sign that he had heard, or was even conscious of his surroundings.

He stood erect, pulling his shoulders back as though he was coming to attention. His eyes were blank, focused on some far distant horizon. He glanced, momentarily, down at the prone form of the Echo and spoke quietly in English.

'Please forgive me, my dear and last friend.'

Bunching his hand into a tight fist, Terrell smashed it downwards with all his strength against the Echo's forehead, just above the eyes. There was a sickening crack of bone as the alien's thin skull imploded like an eggshell, spewing out a fountain of dark blood. Then, as the monitors abruptly went dead, there was a long, terrible moment of utter, shocked silence.

'Forgive me, my friend. Forgive me.'

Terrell was confined to his quarters under close

armed guard – not that it appeared necessary. In the two hours since he had been brought to his room, he had not moved from his bunk. He sat there quietly, his eyes red and ringed from crying.

'Why?' Reece asked, hopelessly, still struggling to understand.

Terrell's voice came from a billion miles away. 'Because he begged me to,' he murmured. 'And because I loved his people.'

He looked up at Amanda beseechingly, seeking understanding. 'It would have been completely painless,' he said. 'There was no suffering. They have a pre-brain there, you see. It processes all functions, but there are no pain receptors.'

'You're claiming that it was a mercy killing,' Reece asked. 'I repeat my question – why?'

'He was the last of his species,' Terrell said, with infinite sadness. 'They're all gone now. They destroyed themselves.'

This information took some time to sink in.

'That explosion we picked up,' Amanda said finally. 'They detonated their own spaceship's engines?'

Terrell's head dropped. 'Not just that one. Every other craft, every other settlement. Their entire civilisation.'

It was almost too much to comprehend.

'Why, man, why?' begged Reece.

'What was it they feared so much?' Drake said, his voice tinged with awe.

'Themselves,' Terrell muttered. 'The nDs were

turning them into their agents. Like your people being given brain implants. The Echoes were a highly compassionate, totally selfless race. They would rather lose their lives than to be put to some violent purpose ... after a fashion we might envy my dead friend.'

He broke off to glance up at Reece. 'Have you ever studied Plato, General? "Only the dead shall see the end of war." '

Reece was unimpressed. 'I'm more concerned about the living. Are you ready to tell us your story now?'

Terrell nodded. 'Yes. I couldn't speak before, for fear of endangering the Echoes. They came once before, to deliver a warning, and we treated them with savagery. They took me among them. I travelled with them, virtually ageless, while more than fifty years of history passed on Earth.'

'What was the warning?' Reece wanted to know.

'Of the nDs,' Terrell said. 'But we weren't ready to listen. They had seen living planets taken throughout the galaxy. The nDs are farmers. They seek out planets with living systems.' He turned his attention to Amanda. 'You were right, Dr Tucker. Their entire civilisation is based upon the manipulation of organic matter. They use the life of a planet as a commodity, a resource, a fuel.'

Drake was aghast. 'And that's how they see us – as farm animals?'

Terrell nodded sombrely. 'Oh yes. Strangely enough, fifty-odd years ago, Earth was their first contact with intelligent beings. So they abducted some people, they studied them and then devised a long-term plan which would enable them to make use of this planet and the curious life form upon it.' He paused briefly. 'They used the water.'

Amanda frowned. 'They put something in our water?'

'Yes,' Terrell said.

Reece snorted with derision and disbelief. 'And that's it? A cosmic war fought by poisoning the water supply?'

Terrell turned to him. 'Oh, no. It was far more subtle than poison,' he continued. 'They used hormones – female hormones.'

Amanda let out a hiss of breath. 'Falling sperm counts,' she said softly.

Both Drake and Reece gave her a quick double-take.

'There have been retrospective studies of medical records,' she went on. 'The average human sperm count has been declining steadily for fifty-odd years. If unchecked, most men will be infertile by the year 2050. The nDs must have put oestrogenic compounds in the world's waters. We thought they came from our own environmental pollution.'

'So they intend to wipe out the human race by making us sterile?' Reece asked.

Terrell shook his head. 'You forget, General. The nDs *use* living things, they don't destroy them. At least, not until they no longer have a useful purpose to fulfil.'

Amanda understood. 'They're feminising us. The birth rate of baby boys is in decline. Gradually, all human beings will be female. In 1944, at the height of the Second World War, that would have seemed logical. It would have appeared males were the sex to eliminate to make us a docile species.'

Drake smiled wryly. 'Sounds like they've still got a lot to learn about women,' he put in. No one was in the mood for humour.

There was one part of all this that Reece still didn't understand. 'But if they intend to use us for some purpose, surely that's a self-defeating strategy,' he pointed out. 'Without men, the human race would die out within a hundred years.'

'That would be more than long enough for the nDs,' Terrell said gravely. 'The Earth would be dead and drained long before then. That's the way they work. They find a world rich with life, they strip it bare, and then they move on.'

'The inter-galactic equivalent of slash-and-burn agriculture,' Amanda breathed. She took a deep breath, staring Terrell in the eye. 'What will they do with us when we're all female?'

Terrell looked wretched. 'I honestly can't say what they have in mind.'

His next statement horrified her. 'I'm afraid you may be the first to know, Dr Tucker.'

Amanda was rocked to the core. Involuntarily, her fingers strayed to her arm, scratching lightly at the wound which still showed no sign of normal healing. nD.

'But if this long-term plan was working – if we were still in the dark and we never got together with the Echoes – then why are they back now?' Drake asked.

Even as the words left his mouth, he realised with an inward sinking feeling that he already knew the answer. Terrell spelled it out for him anyway.

He looked deep into Drake's eyes; an expression of such sadness, such compassion coming over his face. 'When I was shot down, the nDs feared I would pass on the truth to mankind. They failed to capture me before you did. So now they have no other choice but to step up their campaign. They will fight even harder to consume the Earth.'

Terrell paused. 'I'm sorry, Drake – but it was you.'

A terrible, suffocating sense of guilt descended on Drake, rendering him speechless. The consequences of his stupid, arrogant actions – Gerry, Amanda's abduction, Miles, Burton, Friday, the others – the whole Earth – it was all his fault. All his own, reckless doing. It was too much to bear. He was utterly shattered.

Despite her own troubles, Amanda couldn't help feeling for him. She clutched at his arm, squeezing it reassuringly.

'How do we stop them?' Reece wanted to know.

'Charles?' pleaded Amanda.

Terrell shook his head sadly. 'General, the Echoes tried and failed. The nDs are swallowing planet after planet. They're unstoppable.'

Reece refused to accept such defeatism. 'All right, the Echoes are gone,' he conceded. 'But there must be others who can help us. There must be some who have stood against the nDs.'

Terrell was silent for a long while, before delivering the final and most terrible truth of all.

'I'm afraid not,' he muttered at long last. 'Intelligent life is a rarity, rather than the rule in this universe, General. There were only the Echoes, the nDs – and us. There are no others, no chance of help. Earth stands alone now.'

'No.' Reece's voice thundered out in denial. 'I refuse to believe in an invincible enemy. If they're mortal, they can be killed. We just need to know how to fight them.'

'There is no way to fight them,' Terrell said hopelessly. 'They will take your own people and turn them into weapons against you. You'll face a battle on two fronts – both from inside and outside your own ranks. No matter how many nDs you kill, they will simply clone replacements. And all the while, your own planet is working against you. They can't be stopped, General. They come – and they conquer.'

Frustration turned to open anger. Reece turned on Terrell savagely.

'So you're suggesting we do what your Echo friends did?' he demanded bitterly. 'We just give up and commit mass suicide?'

Reece fell silent, and no one else had anything to say.

★ ★ ★

Later that evening, Amanda Tucker sat on the floor alone in her quarters, in silent contemplation of the livid wound on her arm. No longer just red raw, it had started to show signs of a strange tissue growing over it – growing *in* it. Yellow, pus-like tissue.

'Please,' she whimpered. 'Please.' The tears were rolling freely down her face.

There was a tap on the door. Amanda opened it, red-eyed and blotchy, patting down the dressing on her arm again. It was Drake. She turned away and sat at her desk, staring at the framed photograph of Emily.

'You've been crying,' Drake said, simply.

'No, I haven't,' she lied, her back to him. Another tear rolled silently down her cheek.

Drake's heart went out to her. He was desperate to console her.

'Amanda, what Terrell said before . . .' he began awkwardly. 'Look, he was only guessing. He doesn't know. You've been given the all clear by the doctors. Maybe the nDs have spared you. Maybe they've had to change their plans – maybe it's nothing to do with women any more.' It was what Drake desperately wanted to believe.

'Maybe. Maybe. Maybe that's a lot of maybes.'

'But—'

'Let's face it, Chris,' Amanda burst out, turning on him, able to contain herself no longer. 'The nDs farm, feed and make offspring. They don't *feel* for one another. They don't *need* one another.

Maybe theirs is the only way to be to win this war.'

She threw the photograph of her daughter in the bin and turned away again, her head in her hands. 'Now go away.'

Drake stared at her sadly. 'Please, Amanda,' he started.

'Leave me alone.'

As soon Drake had gone, she fished the photograph out of the bin and touched Emily's face through the glass.

'I won't let them get you,' she whispered. 'I won't let them get you.'

CHAPTER ELEVEN

In open countryside, Wing Commander Friday brought the stolen car to a halt by the side of the road. He switched off the engine and climbed out, leaving the ignition key in the lock and the door open. Walking away from the car, he stood for a moment, reviewing the terrain around him through glassy, expressionless eyes.

He looked like a walking corpse – something dragged out of the sea days after drowning. His face and body were grossly bloated, his flesh grey and gangrenous, as though decomposition had already set it. The pockmarks in his face were enlarged and studded with soft yellow pustules of nD tissue. The veins in his neck bulged obscenely, standing out unnaturally dark against his deathly pallor.

Ahead of him, perhaps two miles away, the village of Kirkhaven could be seen as a cluster of red-tiled roofs broken by a single church spire. Closer, to his right, the pale light of dawn glinted on the flat waters of Kirkhaven reservoir.

This, although what was left of his conscious

mind did not realise it, was Friday's destination, and his purpose. The days of lying low, hiding out while his body chemistry worked its programmed metamorphosis, were over.

Zombie-like, Friday turned towards the reservoir and began to walk. There was no urgency in his step, only the coolness of absolute determination. The perimeter fence, topped with barbed wire, presented no obstacle. Friday climbed it with grim resolve, oblivious to the razor-like barbs tearing and lacerating his flesh.

Fully-clothed, he waded into the water until it reached his chest. He rolled up the sleeve of his jacket, exposing his forearm. He reached into his pocket, pulling out a small field medical kit and selecting a scalpel. Then, with cool surgical precision, he made a deep incision into his cubital fossa, revealing the brachial artery. He slashed it lengthways, dropping the scalpel as blood spurted up into his eyes.

His face still without expression, Wing Commander Friday let himself collapse into the reservoir, floating face-down as a dark red cloud spread slowly out into the surrounding water.

In the town, two miles away, the inhabitants were starting to stir. Turning on taps, brushing their teeth, making cups of tea.

Reece and Drake stood by the observation window outside the medical unit. It was now serving as a pathology lab as Preston performed a post-mortem on the dead Echo, assisted by two other experts she had called in.

'This place gets more and more like a base for boffins by the day,' Drake observed, morosely. 'I don't feel I have a place here anymore.'

He waited a few moments to let this sink in. 'With respect, General – I'd like to put on record a formal request that you return me to flying duties, sir.'

Reece grunted. 'Request noted, Drake. You've already got a job here.'

It wasn't the answer Drake wanted to hear. 'But not the job I'm good at,' he protested. 'If this thing blows up in our faces, that's where I'm going to be needed. Dammit, General – we've already been at war for fifty years and we didn't even know it.'

'That's why I need you here,' Reece muttered. 'I'm going to need as many people on my side as I can get.' He paused before explaining himself.

'Look, no one can give me any rational alternative for that explosion we witnessed. They're talking solar flares, exploding comets – all sorts of stuff. But no one *knows* for sure. That's why I'm opening up this operation for inspection. If Terrell's right and Earth stands alone against the nDs, then I need to convince my superiors.'

'And if you can't convince them?' Drake queried.

Reece sighed deeply. 'Then this station stands alone for Earth,' he said dramatically. 'They figure history's written by the victors. If we're beaten, then there might not be any record that man ever existed.'

He gave a helpless shrug. 'Anyway, it's out of my hands now. Air Vice-Marshal Bentley is already on his way here.'

He glanced in through the observation window again. The post-mortem appeared to be over. Group Captain Preston was getting ready to finish up.

'Come on, let's go find out whether we've learned anything new.'

'Well?' Reece asked.

Preston looked slightly harassed. 'I haven't finished my report yet.'

Reece was clearly impatient. 'Preliminary findings will do for now.'

Preston wondered whether to argue for a moment, and decided against it. She picked up her notes, reading them aloud.

'Post-mortem examination conducted by myself, Air Commodore McKenzie, Professor Chiu, Professor Selway. Subject, Echo Uniform Oscar – alleged extraterrestrial of unknown origin.'

Come on, come on, get to the point, Reece thought, but he held his tongue.

'Subject was recovered from a crashed re-entry vehicle, having suffered burns, lacerations and other trauma,' Preston went on. 'Actual cause of death was a blow to the head, causing skull fracture and irreparable brain damage.'

Reece had finally had enough. 'Yes, we already know all that,' he snapped irritably. 'What have we learned?'

Preston faced him coolly. 'The body contained multiple deposits of foreign tissue. Primary analysis would suggest that it has a cellular structure closely allied to, if not identical to, our recovered samples of nD tissue.'

'And what's your interpretation of that?' Reece asked.

Preston chose her words very carefully. 'It might suggest that the nDs were altering the Echoes' physiology. Perhaps making them over in their own image.'

'Backing up Terrell's story – right?' Drake put in.

Preston wasn't willing to go that far. 'Corroborating it, not proving it,' she said cautiously. 'As General Reece requested, these are only the preliminary findings. There's a lot of work to be done yet.'

It was another minor slap on the wrist, but Reece ignored it. 'Thank you, Group Captain,' he said politely. 'I'll await your full report.'

He led the way out of the room to encounter Radcliffe, who snapped to attention. 'Sir, Air Vice-Marshal Bentley is here. He is requesting to see Terrell.'

Reece acknowledged the message with a curt nod. 'I'll see to it.' He turned to Drake. 'Remember what I told you, Drake. I *need* you here. Don't let me down.'

'No sir,' Drake muttered dutifully as Reece strode off.

Radcliffe grinned at him. 'Well, who's the blue-eyed boy all of a sudden?' he asked mockingly. 'I don't think the General's ever used the word "need" to his own wife.'

Drake smiled back, accepting the jibe in the spirit in which it was intended. Nevertheless, it was food for thought.

'Peter – good to see you,' Reece said cordially, extending his hand. He was familiar with Air Vice-Marshal Bentley both by reputation and from personal contact at NATO meetings. He knew the man to be intelligent enough to be open-minded, which was one of the reasons Reece had requested him. He didn't have time to waste on by-the-book pragmatists, of which the service had more than its fair share. Also, Bentley was a former pilot, and could view the crashed escape pod with an objective eye.

Bentley accepted the proffered handshake. 'David,' he acknowledged. First-name terms were acceptable, their respective ranks more or less equal. 'I understand you want me to inspect your command here. Something rather unusual, I believe.'

Reece sniffed. 'You could say that. How much has Squadron Leader Knox already told you?' he asked, glancing quickly over at her.

'Some sort of experimental aircraft of unknown origin. You have the pilot, I believe? I'd like to start with him, if I may.'

'I'll take you to him,' said Knox.

Reece nodded. 'I'll fill you in with the details on the way. I'd like to sit in, if that's OK with you.'

There was no objection. Knox and Reece escorted Bentley to Terrell's quarters.

'So, tell me all about these extraterrestrials of yours,' Bentley said to Terrell after they had all sat down.

'I was taken among them, at my own volition, in 1944,' Terrell started. 'Subjectively, I have aged only a little, since I have been travelling at speeds close to that of light. I have lived among them for more than fifty years, travelled with them to their nearest colony some twenty light years from Earth, and I have studied their language and culture.'

Bentley gave no sign that he either believed or disbelieved.

'And do you have any corroborating evidence to support this story?' he asked politely.

Terrell wasn't sure what he meant. 'I don't understand,' he said.

Bentley smiled. 'Well, photographs, artefacts, that sort of thing.'

Terrell shook his head. 'I wasn't on a sight-seeing trip.'

'But surely, if you visited their planet, you'd have brought back some souvenirs,' Bentley suggested.

There was the faintest suggestion of mockery creeping into Bentley's voice now, and Terrell bristled against it.

'I never visited their home world,' he muttered sullenly. 'It lies too distant. Some of their crews live their entire lifetimes in space without ever even seeing it.'

Bentley was thoughtful for a moment. 'I see.'

He changed tack abruptly. 'You maintain that these people became your friends. You admired them.'

Terrell nodded. 'They were a supremely gentle and wise species. Yes, I admired them.'

'Yet you murdered the individual who supposedly came in response to your distress signal,' Bentley said. His voice had changed suddenly from the interrogative to the accusative. 'Not a very gentle act, was it?'

Terrell looked as though someone had thrust a knife deep into his gut. He lapsed into a depressed silence.

Bentley climbed to his feet, facing Reece. 'Well, shall we go and take a look at this mystery aircraft of yours?' he suggested.

Knox tried to rescue the situation. 'I wonder sir, if you'd like to see the extraterrestrial tissue I mentioned first? We'll pass the science unit on the way to the hangar, and I think it's something you ought to see. Our scientists are working on it at the moment.' She turned to Reece. 'If that's all right with you, sir?'

Reece nodded miserably. The interview with Terrell had not gone smoothly. It did not bode well for the remainder of Peter Bentley's inspection trip.

★ ★ ★

Bentley looked round curiously as he walked into the lab. His interest soon evaporated when he saw the small tubes containing the samples of the yellow nD slime. Reece had to admit they didn't look particularly impressive.

'Is this it?' Bentley asked.

Knox hurried over to talk him through their progression.

Reece called Preston over. 'Is there any way of getting a toxin?' he murmured, hopefully. That would be something to hook Bentley's attention with.

Preston shook her head. 'The tissue we had decomposed within a few hours. There wasn't enough time to test a toxin. I need living flesh.'

Reece stood there, absorbing what he'd been told.

'Living flesh.'

Major General Reece had requested that Drake accompany them to the hangar, on the grounds that he was the only man with flight experience who had managed to make the faintest sense out of the pod's control systems. Sensing that he was really only there as back-up, Drake wisely kept himself in the background.

'So what definite evidence do you have that this vehicle is extraterrestrial in origin?' Bentley demanded.

Reece frowned. He would have thought one look at the craft was answer in itself. 'Its flight systems are far in advance of anything we've got. Hell, we can't even figure out what it's made of. Come on, Peter – *look* at it.'

'I'll tell you what I see, David,' Bentley said calmly. 'I see the strong possibility that one of our rivals has come up with a highly sophisticated and advanced new weapon. And NATO has tasked you with making an appraisal of this new weapon's capabilities.'

Reece gaped at him in disbelief. 'What we have here is something far bigger.'

Bentley shook his head. 'No. What you've got – and I'm playing devil's advocate here because I know how things will look to our bosses – what you've got, David, is a dead freak, a living lunatic and a pile of mangled metal. We're told these "Echoes" conveniently no longer exist, but instead we are under threat from the mystical nDs – the only evidence for which is a few specimen jars of yellow slime.'

Bentley paused for effect. 'I for one fully expect that quite searching questions will be asked about how Major General Reece runs his operation and exactly what he is doing with tax-payers' money.'

He paused again. 'I'm sorry, David, but you asked me for my appraisal and that's it.'

Reece was stunned into silence. The awful thing, he realised, was that Bentley was probably right. In fact, it was probably an under-statement of the way top brass would choose to see things.

Drake could no longer contain himself. 'Begging your pardon, sir,' he said, butting in. 'But three eminent pathologists are going to conclude that the "freak" isn't human. Our own expert has said that the "yellow slime" comes from no creature known on Earth, and we all have enough flying hours between us to take one look at that vehicle and figure out it isn't just some secret prototype.'

'That's enough, Drake,' Knox cut in quickly.

'I think you've said your piece,' Reece nodded.

It amounted to a dismissal. Grudgingly, Drake excused himself and walked off around the side of the hangar.

'What's everybody else doing?' Reece asked.

'The rest of NATO's assuming a more . . . conventional threat. We're covering our airspace and we're looking in all the places you'd expect – satellite reconnaissance of our enemies' flight-test facilities, and so forth. The usual sort of thing.'

'Have you found anything yet?'

'No.' Bentley's look was telling.

'So how do you see it from here?' Reece wanted to know.

The Vice-Marshal pursed his lips thoughtfully. 'Your brief was to study the aircraft – no more. Other departments should be looking at all these other things, not you.'

Reece was openly sceptical. 'You want me to hand everything over so it gets spread across fifteen different commands, all with their heads up their own—'

Bentley's expression was sympathetic, even

friendly. They were colleagues, not adversaries. 'David, you have to stop this,' he counselled.

Reece shook his head vehemently. 'No. I won't. I can't.'

'It could be your career,' Bentley pointed out.

'Then I'm going to have to take that risk,' Reece said firmly. 'I'm not going to put that ahead of my duty to defend us from this threat. I won't. Christ, Peter – this is *happening!*'

'Then prove it,' Bentley said calmly. 'Make us sit up and take notice. Give us something no one can argue with.'

Reece nodded to himself. 'Yeah, maybe I'll do just that,' he muttered darkly.

Bentley glanced at his watch. 'Well, I'd really better be going. Can you have someone arrange transport?'

'Yes, of course,' Reece said. He fell into step a few paces behind Bentley, deep in thought.

So they wanted proof of the nDs' existence, did they? Then he'd give them proof. He'd give them proof that no one could argue with.

Flight Lieutenant Stewart gently removed the dressing from Amanda's arm, exposing her wound. Still not healing normally, the scratched letters *nD* were now marked out against her white flesh by a crusty, yellow scab.

Stewart's eyes narrowed slightly. 'How long has it been like this?'

Amanda tried to appear nonchalant. 'A day or so,' she said vaguely.

She didn't feel nonchalant. In truth, she had been desperately dreading what Stewart and Preston might say ever since the scabby tissue had started to form. It had taken her all day to pluck up the courage to face her fears.

Stewart picked up a scalpel, using the reverse side of the blade to prod the scab delicately.

'Is that sensitive?'

Amanda shook her head. 'No, it feels numb.'

Stewart turned the scalpel over. 'Let's take a sample then, shall we? Take a look at it under a microscope and see exactly what it is.'

He sliced into the crusty top of the raised scab and excised a thin sliver, picking it up carefully with a pair of tweezers and transferring it to a slide.

Amanda looked down at her arm. A small bubble of yellow goo oozed from the place where the scalpel had done its work. Her eyes travelled upwards to meet Stewart's, exchanging a worried look. She was seeking reassurance he couldn't give her.

Silently, Stewart applied a fresh dressing to the wound and touched Amanda lightly on the shoulder. 'I'll let you know the results as soon as I've finished tests,' he told her.

He waited until she had left the room before phoning Preston.

'I think you'd better come and take a look at this,' he said, with a sense of urgency in his voice.

Group Captain Preston raised her head from the eyepiece of the microscope. 'It's nD tissue,' she stated flatly.

Stewart nodded. 'That's what I thought, but I really needed your confirmation.'

Preston was thoughtful for a while. 'The point is – what's it doing on Dr Tucker?'

'It could be just an isolated lesion,' Stewart suggested, not very convincingly. 'Maybe the broken skin of her wound was open to infection in the nD environment.'

'And it could be the same process as we observed in the dead Echo,' Preston pointed out, voicing their mutual fear.

They were both silent for some time, considering the full implications of this statement.

'We'd better call the General,' Stewart said finally, starting to reach for the phone.

'No, wait.' Preston laid her fingers across his arm, restraining him. 'Not before we have access to all the relevant facts. Until then, Dr Tucker is to be accorded the rights of confidentiality we'd give to any ordinary patient.'

Stewart regarded her with mild surprise. Her apparent concern jarred, somehow. The explanation just didn't quite sit right in his mind. There was a hidden agenda in there somewhere.

'Besides,' Preston added, confirming this view. 'It's our best sample of nD tissue so far. 'Enough to test for a toxin. Get straight on to it while I go and see Dr Tucker.'

★ ★ ★

The fact that Preston had made a special trip to see her was ominous in itself, Amanda thought. That she was so obviously and deliberately trying to be reassuring made it doubly so.

'I think it's most likely an infected wound,' Preston was saying. 'Probably no more serious than an abscess or an ulcer.'

'And that's all?' Amanda asked, desperately hoping she was right, wanting so much to believe her.

Preston nodded. 'I think we should be able to remove it easily enough later today. I'll let you know when we're ready for you.'

She gave Amanda a last smile before she left. 'Try not to worry about it too much.'

It was a bit like telling a broody chicken not to lay eggs, Amanda reflected moodily.

Preston made her way back to the medical unit. Stewart looked up as she entered, his face glum.

'You'd better take another look at that tissue sample we took from Dr Tucker,' he murmured, indicating the microscope beside him.

Preston bent over it, bitterly disappointed by what she saw. 'It's decomposed already.'

Stewart nodded miserably. 'Same as last time. There wasn't enough time to test for a toxin. I'm sorry, ma'am.'

Preston looked distant, deeply thoughtful. 'Or maybe there was,' she murmured.

Stewart failed to understand. 'Ma'am?'

Preston's eyes glinted. 'Suppose our atmosphere itself is toxic to them?' she suggested. 'Perhaps they can't survive for long in our environment. That might explain why their incursions have been so brief.'

'And their tissue remains viable only as long as it is grafted on to a human host,' Stewart put in, catching the drift of her argument. 'Like a parasitic growth.'

Preston nodded. 'That might explain a lot of things. Why they need to adapt other living beings. They take a native species and they modify them to support their own genetic structure.'

Stewart was reaching for the phone again, and this time Preston didn't stop him. This was something Major General Reece ought to know about.

Reece had called Preston, Knox and Drake to meet with him. But this seemed like more than a meeting: it was a War Council.

'While we sit back and watch, the nD campaign rolls on,' Reece said heavily. 'It's time to seize the initiative.'

Knox broke in. 'To my mind, seizing the initiative means directing what limited resources we have towards finding out the true threat – that of our enemies here on Earth.'

Reece glanced at Preston. 'What's your view?'

Preston considered her words. 'We know that nD technology is vastly superior to ours,' she said finally. 'But we also know that they're living creatures, they probably can't survive long in our environment, and they can be injured. They do have weaknesses. That makes biological warfare our best hope – possibly our only hope.'

Reece nodded thoughtfully. 'OK, I'll go along with part of that.' He looked to Drake. 'Nothing helpful from Terrell, I suppose?'

Drake shook his head. 'He's still convinced the nDs are unbeatable – but I'm working on him.'

'Good.' Reece fell silent for a moment. 'Seems to me there's only one way to proceed. We've got to capture one of them alive.'

Knox looked doubtful. 'But we don't know what they are, or where they are.'

Only Drake seemed enthusiastic about Reece's suggestion. 'Then we bring them here,' he said brightly.

It was Preston's turn to be openly dubious now. 'We have no idea how to contact them. We don't know how to trap them, and we haven't once been able to contain them,' she pointed out.

'Then we'll find a way,' Drake said.

'Damn right we will,' Reece echoed. 'Everybody seems to be screaming for proof – well there's one sure way to get it.'

Knox wasn't ready to let it go. 'No matter who or what they are – that would mean deliberately breaching our own security. That's inherently dangerous.'

Reece fixed her with a cold gaze. 'I'm fully aware of the risks, Squadron Leader.'

She was still defiant. 'Sir, I strongly advise

against it. You would be putting this station and our staff in needless jeopardy.'

Reece had an answer for that. The only answer, in his book. 'We're at war,' he said simply, as though it was a point she had overlooked. He rose from his seat. As far as he was concerned, the meeting was over.

Knox tried one more time. 'Sir, please – why can't you let this go?'

Reece looked at her intensely. 'If I screw up, you'll get your chance, Squadron Leader Knox. Till then, it's my call and it's my responsibility.'

There was an awkward silence as he left the room. Knox and Preston exchanged furtive glances. It was obvious to Drake that they had their own agenda to discuss.

'I'm going to talk to Terrell,' he said, glad of an excuse to leave them alone.

Preston spoke first. 'There's some biological process occurring in Amanda Tucker,' she announced. 'Foreign tissue is forming in her body.'

Knox looked horrified. 'What's happening to her?'

'At the moment, I'm not sure. I need to study her. I'm removing the tissue later today. Perhaps she should be confined.'

'You believe that to be necessary?'

Preston wasn't quite ready to be drawn into a definitive position. 'Let's put it this way – when the other abductees were considered to be security risks, all were confined except her.'

'General Reece felt her contribution to this project was too valuable to be lost,' Knox pointed out.

Preston was silent for a while. When she spoke again, her voice had taken on a franker quality.

'You and I might have disputed the exact nature of our enemy, but I think we're in complete agreement on how enormous a security risk it is to lure the nDs here. Even more so, perhaps, with someone on the loose who could be connected to them.'

It was Knox's turn to be reflective. There was more to the conversation than met the eye. Susan Preston was verbally fencing with her, she was sure.

'Why are you telling me this? Why not take it straight to the General?' she asked cautiously.

Preston decided that it was time to come clean. She took a deep breath and put her cards on the table.

'Because it's pretty clear to me that if this attempt goes wrong, this will be your command, not his,' she said, plainly. 'I thought it might be a good idea if you and I understood one another.'

Drake had outlined Reece's plan of trapping an nD to Terrell, who looked aghast at the concept.

'It's madness. You'd be like lambs to the slaughter.'

Drake found the man's continuing defeatism annoying. 'We know they have weaknesses,' he said testily. 'They can't be invincible beings. If we can only trap one, we'll be able to find ways of killing them in large enough numbers.'

Terrell was mocking. 'Large enough numbers for what?'

'To beat them,' Drake snapped. His anger was rising to the surface. 'That's not a word in your vocabulary, is it, Terrell? Your Army file still has you charged with desertion. You were away for over fifty years – fifty years in which the nDs plotted against us and you knew about it. Did it really take you that long to study the Echoes' formula for lasting peace and harmony or was it just another example of you having no stomach for battle?'

The attempt to goad the man into a show of aggression failed. Terrell merely smiled sadly.

'I returned when it was my time to help. And you attacked me without provocation, just as you attacked those who brought you a warning. You've sent me crashing into this war that you've brought upon yourselves. You've learned nothing in fifty years. *Nothing*. I'd hoped that I could change him, but now I see that by his very nature, Man is driven to war and his own destruction.'

There was nothing left to do except plead, so Drake pleaded.

'Then help us, Charles. Help us survive this so we *can* have peace one day. Help us make up for our mistakes.'

He paused, and looked deep into Terrell's eyes. 'Please. Help me make up for *my* mistake.'

There was no response.

'It's madness,' Terrell repeated hopelessly. 'They'll come and they'll take us all – you and me and everyone else on this station. You won't beat them. You can't beat them.'

CHAPTER TWELVE

The next day was an unusual one for Kirkhaven's local GP. He generally did a lot of reading during his working day. The small town's population was hardly large enough to merit a medical practice at all, and most of them were typically hardy Scots country folk anyway. Apart from treating the odd bout of flu or delivering babies, he had a lot of time on his hands.

Today, however, his latest novel still lay unopened and unread in his briefcase. There had been a steady trickle of patients through the doors ever since the surgery had opened at 8.30 that morning. All registering the same symptoms. Diarrhoea mostly. Hot flushes, bouts of giddiness, a general feeling of weakness. Temperatures surprisingly normal.

He escorted his present patient to the door. Opening it, he could see that the waiting room was full to bursting point. Behind the desk, his receptionist was looking increasingly stressed. She threw him a harassed glance.

'All the same symptoms?' he whispered to her.

She nodded. 'And I've had at least another dozen on the phone, complaining they're too sick to get into the surgery. What is it, Doctor?'

'I'm not sure,' he admitted. 'But if it's what I think it is, we're going to need help down here.' He pursed his lips thoughtfully for a few moments. 'Hold all patients for a few minutes,' he murmured eventually. 'I have to make a phone call.'

The doctor returned to his consulting room, extracting a small blue file from his desk drawer and consulting it. He reached for the telephone, dialling a number.

'Hello, I need to speak to the Director of Public Health right away. Yes, it's an outbreak, possibly food poisoning.'

Amanda regarded the wound on her arm with sick revulsion, fighting an impulse to shudder. The entire scab had been surgically removed less than a day earlier but it had already reformed, growing back in her flesh like some filthy alien parasite. The letters nD were no longer visible under the crusted yellow tissue, which had now grown to the size and appearance of a fat, pallid, garden slug.

Amanda tore her eyes away from the loathsome thing, pressing the dressing back into place over it. With a low, sinking feeling in the pit of her belly, she set out for the medical unit for her now daily check-up.

Group Captain Preston inspected the growth

with cool detachment, showing no outward sign of concern. Amanda found this in itself disconcerting, even menacing.

'Why? Why would it grow back?' she pleaded.

It was clear she desperately needed an answer, Preston realised. Any kind of answer. She chose her words carefully.

'I can only give you an example of another condition. There's a disease called sarcoidosis. It resembles TB.'

'But that's internal,' Amanda interrupted, increasingly agitated.

Preston tried to sound comforting. 'True, but a curious feature is that, although it mainly affects the lungs and other internal organs, if a patient has old scar tissue on his or her skin, then sarcoid tissue can sometimes appear in the scar. Perhaps this is a similar phenomenon.'

The answer did nothing to dispel Amanda's fears. There was an obvious implication, she concluded. There was a distinct quaver in her voice as she spoke again.

'Are you telling me that this is only an outward manifestation? That there might be tissue like this developing inside me as well?'

Preston suspected her patient was on the edge of hysteria and felt slightly out of control herself. She was a medical scientist, not a GP, and her bedside manner left much to be desired at the best of times. Unable to cope, she needed back-up. 'I think we ought to have someone else in on this.' She thumbed the intercom on her desk.

'Squadron Leader Knox – could you please report to the medical wing at once.'

She returned her attention to Amanda, assuming a purely defensive position of professional detachment.

'I can't say how far the metamorphosis is going to progress. Indeed, it may have reached its final stage already.'

She had underestimated Amanda's powers of self-control. Faced with the final revelation, she seemed to pull herself together, find inner reserves. '*Metamorphosis*. I'm changing, aren't I?' she asked, with deliberate calm. 'Am I becoming one of them?'

Preston faced her with a level gaze. 'I'm afraid I can't say. No one can,' she muttered flatly.

There was a long silence, broken eventually by Knox's entrance. She regarded Susan Preston curiously.

'Well?'

'In view of our experience with Friday and the others, I have reservations about Dr Tucker's continuing participation in this operation,' Preston announced.

Knox could see Amanda was about to protest, and forestalled it. 'Perhaps it would be best if you voluntarily removed yourself from duty and placed yourself under full-time medical care,' she suggested.

Amanda hadn't missed the subtle interchange between the two women as Knox had entered the room. There was something going on between them. Amanda suspected some hidden agenda.

'I have no implant. I'm free of nD control. General Reece wants me on this project,' she said pointedly. 'Perhaps we ought to consult him – or is he no longer making decisions around here?'

She stared directly at Knox as she spoke. It was a challenge, which the women could not meet. She averted her eyes.

'Amanda, show some sense. This is a highly sensitive project, already in some jeopardy.'

Amanda's eyes blazed with defiance. 'I solve problems. I don't add to them.'

'Is that really the case?' Preston queried. 'Haven't you continually drawn conclusions which only serve to justify your role here?'

'Facts have led me to those conclusions,' Amanda said, quietly but forcefully.

It was Knox's turn. 'Some of the ideas you've put into General Reece's head have made him seriously neglect the security of this station. Perhaps your connection with the nDs is far stronger than a mere belief in their existence.'

Amanda flashed her a contemptuous glance. 'I doubt the nDs are bickering among themselves right now. It's not me you should be scared of, it's them. So right now, I'm going back to my work to try and stop them destroying us.'

She stormed out of the medical wing, leaving the two women alone.

Knox repeated her earlier question. 'Well?'

Susan Preston sighed deeply. 'Before Dr Tucker

came in here this morning, I was studying the results of her latest tests. She's changing.'

'Changing? How?'

'Scans all show subtle changes in the structure of her internal organs. Her blood tests are wildly abnormal. I suspect this is the start of an ongoing process that could transform her entire body. Quite into what, or how quickly, I can't say at present.'

Knox looked utterly horrified. 'Does this mean she could go the way of Friday?'

'Possibly,' Preston confirmed with a curt nod, unwilling to be any more definite.

Knox was thoughtful for a moment. 'But Friday had a brain implant, and we know Dr Tucker doesn't,' she pointed out.

This was something Preston had already given considerable thought to. 'Perhaps the implants were just a crude, temporary measure. What's happening in Dr Tucker may be a more sophisticated, long-term method of control. We have no way of knowing how these internal changes may go on to affect her mental state.'

'Does she know?' Knox asked.

Preston shook her head. 'Not at the moment. Not for sure, anyway. But I think she's already beginning to suspect.'

'Treatment?' Knox asked.

Preston frowned. 'I don't think there's anything we can do. Perhaps the best we can hope for is to scrutinise a new phenomenon, observe its progress and anticipate its outcome. Meanwhile, we might be able to exploit this opportunity to manufacture our best hope of defeating the nDs.'

Knox didn't understand. 'I don't follow you, ma'am.'

Preston regarded her with mild surprise. She thought her meaning would have been obvious.

'So far our efforts to develop a biological weapon against the nDs have been frustrated by a lack of living nD flesh. It would appear that is about to change,' she said calmly.

She was completely unprepared for the look of shock which registered on Knox's face.

'I'm an officer first, a scientist second and a doctor third,' she added quickly, trying to justify herself. 'I have to consider any opportunity which presents itself in that order.'

She knew even as she spoke that she had failed to make her case. Helen Knox was staring at her with undisguised contempt. The tentative bond of understanding which had been established between them was broken for ever.

'I'm taking this to General Reece,' Knox announced finally.

Preston still wasn't quite sure where she had gone wrong.

'Why?' she asked.

Knox sighed. 'Because, Group Captain Preston, Amanda Tucker's right. If we don't all start pulling together we're doing the nDs' job for them. And because we need Amanda now more than ever – and she needs our support.'

Major General Reece still seemed set on his plan to trap a live nD. Of this, Knox was still dubious, but she'd committed herself to full support now and there was no going back.

'I hope you understand, General,' she said quietly, humbly. 'I might not have shown you all the confidence you deserved, earlier – but things are different now. It might not mean much, sir – but we're all in this thing together.'

Reece nodded understandingly. 'Thanks, Helen. Actually, it means quite a lot.'

'Anything I can do, sir?' she asked.

Reece thought for a moment, finally shaking his head. 'I think we're doing just about everything we can. Before we can actually trap an nD, we've got to find a way of attracting them here – but on our initiative, not theirs. Drake and Dr Tucker are working on the communications system of Terrell's pod. If we can crack that, maybe we can send out a signal which will get their attention.'

There was a tap at the door.

'Come,' Reece called.

Radcliffe strode in. His face was grim.

'Sir, the civilian police have found Wing Commander Friday's body. I've arranged for it to be brought back here.'

Reece accepted the news philosophically. He had not for one second imagined that they would find Friday alive. 'Where did they find him?' he wanted to know.

'Floating in Kirkhaven reservoir,' Radcliffe

said. 'The police are calling it "the vampire slaying". Every drop of blood was drained from his body.'

'Kirkhaven,' Knox muttered thoughtfully. 'Wasn't that where the nDs returned our people after the abduction?'

Radcliffe nodded. 'Yes ma'am.'

Reece looked up from his desk. 'Are you thinking there may be some kind of connection?'

'Perhaps even more,' Knox said, darkly. 'There have been three incursions into our space by the nDs so far. Two were here, apparently guided in by the homing beacon device in Terrell's tooth. That suggests that they need some sort of a signal to beam in on. The only other one we know about was just outside Kirkhaven, to deliver us back our people.'

Reece was getting the gist of her argument. 'You're suggesting that they have some kind of base there?'

Knox pulled the facial equivalent of a shrug. 'Or a contact,' she muttered.

Reece directed himself to Radcliffe. 'Take a couple of men and get up there,' he ordered. 'Contact the local police, find out what you can. Check out any strange reports over the past few weeks.'

'What are we looking for, sir?' Radcliffe wanted to know.

Reece told him the plain truth. 'I don't really know,' he admitted. 'But maybe we'll recognise it if we see it.'

Radcliffe turned to leave. Knox called after him, an afterthought. 'Oh, and before you go, ask Amanda Tucker to join us in the pathology lab as soon as Friday's body is brought in, will you?'

Amanda wrinkled her nose with disgust at the sight and smell of Friday's bloated, naked body.

Preston was unmoved. 'Well, he's not going to be too fragrant, is he? He was probably in the water for at least two days.' She probed Friday's deeply pockmarked face with a pair of fine surgical tweezers, picking at the studs of scabby nD tissue embedded in them. 'Apart from these, there are no outward physical signs of bodily change, but I'll probably know more when we've opened him up.'

This statement was perfectly true. With the draining of his blood, and subsequent immersion in the water, Friday's corpse had lost the plethoric appearance it had taken on in the last few hours of his life. Preston turned her attention to the direct cause of his death.

'The soft tissues of the antecubital fossa have been carefully dissected,' she announced. 'The brachial artery has been opened with surgical precision by someone who knew exactly what they were doing and had the right tools for the job. A surgical scalpel, I'd say – and from the angle of incision, most probably self-inflicted.'

Amanda shuddered suddenly. The thought of someone sufficiently crazed to slice open their own flesh filled her with horror. Ironic, given the nature of her own self-inflicted wound.

'The choice of wound was obviously designed to release as much blood as possible while the heart was still beating,' Preston continued. 'From the lack of bloodstains on the rest of his body and clothing, he was probably already in the water when he did it.'

'But why?' Reece asked, baffled.

Amanda was pretty sure she had the answer.

'The nDs used him as a biological bomb,' she said quietly. 'They infected him with something which developed and multiplied in his blood-stream and programmed him to release it into a public water supply.' She looked up at Reece with anguish on her face. 'General – Terrell told us the nDs use living creatures for their own ends. Now we have an idea of just what they're capable of.'

Preston agreed. 'Dr Tucker's probably right. It's the only explanation which makes any logical sense. It's quite probable that your other two men were programmed to do the same thing somewhere else, had they survived.'

Reece looked as though he was going to be sick. 'Jesus,' he breathed disgustedly. 'What kind of an enemy are we taking on here?'

Out of a sense of duty, Reece had accepted Preston's invitation to attend the full post-mortem on Friday's body scheduled for that after-noon. He averted his eyes as she lifted off the top of the man's skull and began to pull out his brain.

Radcliffe's urgent tapping on the outside of the observation window came as an extremely welcome diversion. Reece excused himself and stepped outside. Radcliffe looked uncharacteristically morose.

'Sorry to disturb you, sir – but I thought it was important. You were right about Kirkhaven, General. There *is* something weird going on down there.'

Reece's ears pricked up. 'Weird?'

'Some kind of epidemic, sir. Apparently half the village is infected. The local GP has already called in the Public Health Department.'

Reece exhaled a long, deep sigh. It looked like his worst fears were coming true. Tucker had been right. 'Anything else?'

Radcliffe nodded gravely. 'Yes sir. A couple of people reported a strange occurrence at the home of one of their neighbours. They spoke of blinding white lights, a funny crackling sound – sound familiar?'

The question didn't need an answer. 'This neighbour – did you speak to him?'

'Her. She's gone, sir,' Radcliffe answered, with a shake of his head. 'There were scorchmarks just inside the kitchen door and part of the lino was melted. Looks like the nDs took her.'

Reece sighed again. 'All right, Flight Lieutenant. You were right to disturb me. You'd better take a bigger detachment of men, get back there and place a guard on the house. But the first sign of nD activity and you pull back, you understand? No gung-ho heroics. I can't afford to lose any more good men.'

Radcliffe nodded. 'Understood sir.' He was about to turn and leave when another thought struck him. 'Begging your pardon, sir – but there was another strange thing about that village. I've never seen so many girls in one small place before.'

Reece's expression was faintly admonishing. 'Hardly the time to be thinking about your sex life, Flight Lieutenant.'

The General had misunderstood, Radcliffe realised. He hastened to explain himself. 'No, sir – what I mean is all the children, all the young people in the village. They were nearly all girls, sir. As though just about every child born there over the last twenty years or so had been female. It just seemed ... well, kind of odd, sir.'

Reece frowned thoughtfully, recalling one of Amanda Tucker's earlier theories about the nDs. *'They're feminising us. Gradually, all human beings will be female.'*

He pulled his mind back to the present, reviewing the wider issue. It was beginning to look increasingly as though his own theory was also right – that the nDs had already established some sort of terrestrial base in Kirkhaven. It made sense. These tiny Scottish villages were isolated and fiercely parochial.

Like little vacuums within the communication systems of the outside world. News was slow to get in, slow to get out. What better sort of place to work quietly and secretly, unseen and unsuspected, over a number of years?

Reece suddenly realised that Radcliffe was still standing there, waiting uncertainly for further orders. 'All right, carry on.' Reece muttered, dismissing him. Still deep in thought, he walked back into the makeshift pathology lab.

Group Captain Preston had most of Friday's major organs removed and laid out in various receptacles and measuring devices. She looked up at Reece as he returned.

'This was more than just a brain implant,' she announced. 'Friday's whole body was being transformed.' She broke off to indicate the removed liver and spleen, like a butcher pointing out his choice cuts of the day. 'Both grossly enlarged, unusually heavy.'

'Reason?' Reece asked.

Preston looked perplexed. 'General, I'm not even sure of the cause. But at a guess, I'd say that his body was being made to produce as much blood as possible. That fits with our findings here, and might explain why he was made to bleed to death. His blood was the important thing.'

Which once again tied in with Amanda's idea of Friday being used as a biological bomb, Reece thought.

'Have you managed to isolate anything?'

'Flight Lieutenant Stewart's working on it now,' Preston told him. 'Blood loss wasn't total – there were some residual clots in the right ventricle. That should tell us what was so precious about his blood.'

Almost on cue, Stewart appeared from one of the adjoining rooms, carrying a computer print-out.

'You were right,' he told Preston. 'There is an agent present in Friday's blood. It's not a bacterium, virus or prion. It's something else, an entirely unknown species.'

'And now it's in the Kirkhaven water supply,' Reece said heavily. 'And infecting most of the local population.'

This was a new development as far as Preston was concerned. She looked at Reece in alarm. 'This thing is loose?'

Reece nodded gravely. 'I'm afraid so. The entire village seems to be in the grip of an epidemic. The local doctor thinks it's food poisoning.'

Preston's lips curled into a thin smile. 'Poor fool. He won't have the faintest idea of what he's dealing with. I'd better talk to him, find out what the symptoms are and how serious it is.'

'Yeah. That might be a good idea,' Reece muttered. He turned and walked away, heading for his office, damning Air Vice-Marshal Bentley under his breath. He'd wanted proof. Now he had a crisis.

His return to Kirkhaven was even stranger than the first visit, Radcliffe thought. The small convoy of military jeeps had cruised into the centre of the village without encountering a single other vehicle. The place itself was like a little ghost town, with shops closed and an all-pervasive air of abandonment. There was hardly anybody on the streets, and the few locals Radcliffe did observe appeared to be walking awkwardly, as though in pain.

'Jesus, this place gives me the creeps,' Sergeant Tuffley observed, putting into words what they all felt.

They came to a small row of cottages. A few curtains moved suspiciously as they passed, but there was no other sign of life. In the lead jeep, Radcliffe signalled the convoy to a halt across the street from the missing woman's home. He stood up, turning to address the rest of the men.

'Right, we surround the house, take up defensive posit—'

He never got to finish the sentence. The portal opened without the initial crackle of energy which had occurred in the past. It was more immediate, more precise, Radcliffe reflected briefly – as though an established circuit had merely been switched on again. The windows of the little cottage blazed with bright light, as if floodlit from within. The walls bulged, then contracted again, the exterior plumbing pipes writhing into serpent-like shapes.

Some of the airmen were already bundling out of the jeeps, cocking their weapons. Sergeant Tuffley was more cautious.

'Do we go in?' he screamed at Radcliffe, nervously.

'No!' Radcliffe's urgent shout was as much a warning as it was a command. 'General Reece ordered us to hold back if there was any nD activity. Everyone take immediate cover.' He put his own words into practice, jumping out of the jeep and taking shelter behind it. He waited until the light began to fade before peering cautiously over the top again. 'Right – now we go in.'

The kitchen door was unlocked, as it had been on his first visit. Radcliffe threw it open, covering the interior with his assault rifle.

The portal had not quite finished closing. A roughly oval-shaped pool of distortion surrounded a woman's prone form, contorted foetuslike on the kitchen floor. A long, thin and fleshy-looking cannula, looking like a bloated tapeworm, extended from the woman's jugular vein and stretched into the void.

As Radcliffe stared at it in disgust, the thing detached itself with a faint plopping sound, leaving a small trickle of blood on the woman's neck. Writhing obscenely, it slithered back into the diminishing portal and was gone. The portal finally closed in complete silence, leaving behind the distinctive reek of melted plastic.

Radcliffe bent over the motionless body of the woman, fully expecting her to be dead. She opened her eyes suddenly, making him jump. There was a dreamy smile on her face as she came to full consciousness and began climbing to her feet. She stared at Radcliffe and the other armed airmen with detached curiosity.

'Who are you? What are you all doing in my house?' she demanded finally, as the smile faded from her face.

Radcliffe fussed around her concernedly. 'Are you all right, ma'am?'

She began to look indignant. 'Of course I'm all right. Why shouldn't I be? Now please tell me what you're doing here.'

Radcliffe waved it aside. 'Later, ma'am. I'll explain everything to you later. Now, what did they do to you?'

The woman looked blank. 'What has who done to me?'

It was clear she had absolutely no idea of what had happened to her, Radcliffe realised. The nDs had obviously learned from their earlier experience with Friday and the others. Now they were injecting their victims with some kind of memory suppressant. Probably a tranquilliser, too, judging from the woman's outwardly calm demeanour.

He took her arm gently. 'I think you'd better sit down, ma'am,' he suggested. 'I think it would be a good idea to have our medical team check you over.'

Group Captain Susan Preston and Flight Lieutenant Stewart had been down to Kirkhaven to check out the abducted woman. Their report to

Major General Reece was bizarre, to say the least.

'So, she doesn't appear to have been seriously harmed?' Reece asked.

'Quite the contrary, in fact,' Preston agreed. 'When I spoke to the local doctor, he told me she was a very sick woman. Right now, she appears to be in the rudest of health.'

'So what have the nDs done to her?' Reece wanted to know.

Stewart stepped forward. 'Sir, there are puncture marks in her jugular veins, subclavians and femorals.'

He might as well have been speaking Chinese to Reece. 'Which means, exactly?'

Preston translated. 'Someone – or something – has accessed all her great veins,' she said. 'One might speculate that they were drawing off her blood.

'What about her blood itself?' Amanda asked. 'Is there anything abnormal about it?'

Stewart nodded. 'Very highly raised urine 5-hydroxyindole-acid levels. Usually a sign of carcinoid syndrome, although that was not one of the symptoms which the GP reported in any of the victims so far.'

Reece was rapidly getting completely out of his depth. 'Are you trying to tell me the nDs have cured her of one disease and given her another instead?'

Preston didn't give him an answer, simply because she didn't have one herself.

'My knowledge of organic chemistry is pretty limited,' Amanda murmured cautiously. 'But aren't we talking about serotonin here?'

Preston raised one eyebrow, obviously impressed. 'Yes,' she admitted. 'Carcinoid syndrome is a tumour of the intestine which secretes large quantities of serotonin into the bloodstream.'

'And serotonin is?' Reece prompted, struggling to keep up and wishing that he'd paid more attention to chemistry lessons at college.

'Serotonin is a natural bio-chemical substance secreted by the human body and used by the brain and nervous system as a chemical transmitter,' Amanda informed him.

Preston elaborated. 'It's usually produced naturally in the body from existing stores of tryptophan. Depletion of those stores would cause pellagra, resulting in the skin damage. On the other hand, excessive over-production of serotonin would cause the subject to become extremely ill – probably exhibiting much the same symptoms as those reported by the local GP.'

'And like this woman had,' Amanda put in.

Preston nodded.

Amanda was thoughtful for a few seconds. 'But now she's better, apparently cured.'

Susan Preston hastened to clear up a point. 'I never said she was cured. I merely observed that at the moment, she appears to be in good health. If her body continues to over-produce serotonin, she will very quickly become ill again.'

Major General Reece was starting to see an

overall pattern. 'So the nDs introduce a disease which makes people ill, but doesn't kill them. Then they abduct the victim, clear up the symptoms and then return them to become sick again. But how? Why? It doesn't make sense.'

'Perhaps it does,' Amanda said suddenly, her voice strangely chilled. 'Their kind of sense, anyway.' She turned her attention back to Susan Preston. 'Suppose they were merely filtering off that excess serotonin – perhaps in a similar way to how waste products in the bloodstream can be removed by dialysis.'

'That would certainly explain the puncture marks in the veins,' Stewart put in. Susan Preston said nothing.

'And then the victim is returned to manufacture more serotonin,' Amanda went on. 'Doesn't that remind any of you of something. Haven't you ever seen a herd of cows led into the milking shed?' Amanda asked. 'Drained of their milk and then returned to pasture until their udders are full again?'

The analogy struck home. Reece's jaw dropped as the final sickening realisation hit him. 'They're farming us – like dumb animals,' he breathed, horrified. There was still one thing he didn't quite understand. 'But what's so damned valuable about serotonin?'

Susan Preston spoke up, fitting another piece into the puzzle. 'We know the nDs are purely a biotechnology. Their machines are living matter. Muscle in the place of metal, bone instead of concrete – neural networks in the place of wiring circuits. And as Amanda already explained, serotonin is a chemical transmitter.'

Reece thought he had the picture, but he needed clarification. 'You're saying they need this stuff to run their machines?'

Preston nodded gravely. 'It could be that serotonin is as fundamentally important to their industry and technology as oil is to ours.'

There was a long silence as they all digested this shattering theory. Finally, Reece noticed that Amanda was trembling. Her face was pale, wearing a haunted expression as though she had just realised one last horror that no one else had thought of.

'What is it?' he asked gently.

Tears pricked at the corners of Amanda's eyes. 'Absentee farmers,' she murmured distantly. 'The nDs can't keep coming here to filter off the serotonin. It takes them too much energy and effort. And they won't be able to settle here themselves because they can't survive in our environment. So they're going to need someone to mind the farm. They'll need to create shepherds.'

She fell silent, unbuttoning the cuff of her blouse. She rolled up the sleeve, finally unpeeling the wound dressing and thrusting her arm forward for Preston's inspection.

The nD stigma had increased in size quite noticeably since the last examination. Outwardly, it now extended almost to Amanda's wrist. Around its edges, a further corona of yellow growth could be observed beneath the normal skin.

Susan Preston was acutely and uncomfortably aware of Amanda's eyes boring into hers. They were terrified, pleading.

'Is that what this is all about?' Amanda asked, a sob catching at her voice. 'Was this what they planned from the start – to turn me into some sort of hybrid slave to do their filthy work for them?'

They were questions which begged a denial. A denial that Preston couldn't offer her.

'I'm sorry, Amanda. I don't know,' she murmured honestly. She could only stare helplessly after the distraught woman as she turned and ran from the room before she broke down completely.

After a long silence, Preston looked up at Reece. 'I told you earlier that she suspected,' she muttered sombrely. 'Now she knows. I'm not sure that she'll be able to cope with it. I'm not sure that anyone could cope with it.'

Reece's face was clouded with depression. 'Yeah,' he grunted. He paced up and down the room as frustration built up inside him in sickening pulses, finally erupting into anger. He stopped in his tracks, whirling on the two medics.

'Dammit – there must be *something* you can do,' he thundered. 'Is there no way to control the process, maybe even reverse it?'

Preston shook her head regretfully. 'We're working on a toxin with the limited resources we have, but we've no real way of testing it. There's too much we don't understand about the nDs – their physical structure, metabolism, body chemistry. And Dr Tucker is way beyond surgery, I'm afraid – even if I thought for a moment that might work.'

Determination blazed in Major General Reece's eyes. 'Then it's even more important that we capture one for study. Find out how to kill the damned things and maybe we'll find a way to kill off that stuff growing in Amanda Tucker's body.'

Reece broke off, aware that both Preston and Stewart were staring at him strangely. For some unknown reason, he felt the need to justify himself.

'Dammit – that might just be the only way we can win this war. Use them the way they're using us. Without pity, without scruples.'

There was no argument.

After leaving the medical wing, Amanda returned to her quarters just long enough to compose herself and touch up her ravaged make-up. Sitting alone and feeling sorry for herself wasn't going to help. She needed to immerse herself in her work, feel that she was actually doing something against the hated nDs which might actually contribute to their eventual defeat.

Besides, that work would inevitably bring her into close contact with Drake, and right now Amanda needed the comfort of a friend more than she'd ever needed anything in her life. She set off for the hangar.

'Just the girl I wanted to see. I could use some help.'

Amanda wriggled into the tight confines of the pod beside him, taking comfort from the body contact.

'It might help me to help you if I knew what you were doing.'

Drake struggled to sit up. 'Just a theory, but I figure this pod gives us our best chance of luring the nDs into a trap. If I can isolate its transmitter and remove it, maybe we can send out a signal which will bring them to source.'

It sounded hopeful, Amanda thought, and said so. 'So, what do you want me to do?' she asked.

Drake nodded towards a small pile of tools by Amanda's side. 'For a start, you can pass me that pair of pincers.'

Amanda's eyes widened in surprise. 'Pincers? Bit low-tech, isn't it?'

Drake grinned sheepishly. 'Yeah, well, the Echoes seem to have had mechanical genius for assembling components without screws. Trouble is, they didn't leave any instructions for taking them apart again.'

Amanda passed the pliers, brushing his fingers with her own. Suddenly Drake was pulling her over into an embrace.

She didn't resist as his lips closed over hers. More than just the physical attraction she had always felt for the man, she desperately needed to feel like a normal woman again. The kiss became more passionate, Drake's tongue exploring the inside of her mouth. For several seconds, she responded, enjoying the surge of hormones through her body.

Drake's heart flipped over in his chest. Nothing he'd ever felt before, no other woman had ever come close to –

Then Amanda pulled back abruptly, turning her face away from his.

Drake was silent for a while. 'What's the matter?' he asked finally, sounding a little puzzled, a little scared.

Amanda was tongue-tied, unable to explain.

Drake reached for her hand, squeezing it. His face was suddenly serious again.

'Really, Amanda – what's the matter?'

She couldn't tell him – explain that she felt incapable of surrendering a body which wasn't fully hers any more. In her mind's eye, she could imagine his revulsion if he realised he was making love to some hideous, alien thing. She couldn't bear to see him recoil from her, to see the abhorrence in his eyes reflecting the disgust she felt for herself. It seemed kinder to lie – for both their sakes.

'I just can't. We've got work to do, remember? The nDs—'

The mere mention of the dreaded name seemed to do it. 'Yeah, right,' Drake sighed, returning his attention to the control panel he had been working on. He wrenched off the face plate, exposing a hideously complicated mass of wiring and circuitry. He stared at it miserably for several moments, knowing he was hopelessly out of his depth.

'What now?' he muttered finally. It wasn't really a question.

Amanda rolled over to take a look for herself. Even to her trained scientific mind, the circuitry showed no discernible pattern or purpose. Like Drake, she was completely baffled.

'There's only one man who can make any sense out of this,' she said at last. 'We need Terrell.'

Drake shrugged resignedly. 'And Terrell steadfastly refuses to co-operate,' he pointed out. 'So that's it – we're beaten.'

Amanda was beginning to extricate herself from the cramped cockpit. Drake frowned. 'Where are you going?'

Amanda pulled herself to her feet outside the pod. She bent down to peer in at Drake again. There was a determined expression on her face. 'I'm going to see him,' she announced. 'Sooner or later, someone has to pull him down from that fence he's been sitting on.'

Finding Terrell wasn't difficult. Ever since the death of the Echoes, he had more or less confined himself to solitary mourning, rarely venturing outside his quarters.

Amanda tapped lightly on his door. 'It's Amanda Tucker. Can I come in, please?'

'Of course.' Terrell glanced up from the book he

was reading as Amanda entered. 'A social visit, Dr Tucker?'

There was no point in beating about the bush. Amanda fixed him with a cool, determined stare. 'Charles, I've come to ask you again if you'll help us.'

Terrell sighed, laying down his book. 'And I've given you all my answer a dozen times. I'm sorry.'

Uninvited, Amanda sat herself down in a spare chair, eyeing him silently for a while.

'Charles, the last Echo – the one who came here – he meant something to you, didn't he?' she murmured finally.

Terrell gave a start of surprise. 'What makes you say that?'

'You called him your dear and last friend,' Amanda said simply. 'And I think that what you did was an act of love.' She paused for a long moment. 'What was his name, Charles?'

A thin, wistful smile played over Terrell's lips. 'The Echoes don't – didn't – have names. They had signatures.'

'Signatures?'

Terrell nodded. 'We have them too, but we don't recognise them. They're what some psychics and clairvoyants refer to as auras – the personal identifying characteristic of all living things.'

'And you? What was your "signature"?' Amanda asked gently.

Terrell's smile was bitter now. 'For many years, my signature was "Death". The Echoes supposed it was something all humans carried – like an invisible mark of Cain.'

He broke off to regard her curiously. 'Why are you asking me these questions?'

'Because I have people who are special to me, too,' Amanda answered. 'Chris Drake, my daughter.'

Again, a flicker of surprise showed in Terrell's eyes. 'You have a daughter? I didn't know.'

'Her name is Emily. She's ten years old. Ten years in which I've watched her grow up, loved her, made plans for her future. Only without your help she doesn't have a future, does she Charles?'

Terrell looked hurt. 'That's unfair. There's nothing I can do.'

'Is it?' Amanda demanded. She was becoming more aggressive now. 'How can you know if you're not prepared to try? How can you be so convinced that the nDs are unbeatable if you won't help us to stand against them?'

For the first time, Amanda saw the shadow of doubt on Terrell's face. She pressed home the advantage. 'Think it through, Charles. You gave up any chance of a normal life to bring us lasting peace. You know the nDs will never let us have that unless we're prepared to fight back.'

'And afterwards?' Terrell asked. 'Suppose Man has survived? Who then saves him from himself?'

Amanda reached out and touched his hand. 'That's Man's problem, not yours,' she said gently. 'Just give us the chance to work it out for ourselves.'

Terrell shook his head uncertainly, caught hopelessly in the eternal dilemma between ideology and humanitarianism. 'I don't know.'

Sensing victory, Amanda kept up the pressure.

'Man is not like the Echoes, Charles. Perhaps he isn't so noble, quite so selfless. And, yes, he is an aggressive species – but if that's a weakness, then maybe it can be our only strength as well. The Echoes failed to beat the nDs and gave up. We won't do that, because as a species we *can't* give up, it's not in our nature. If anyone can stop the nDs, it's us.'

Amanda had one final card – quite literally – up her sleeve. She peeled back the dressing on her arm for the second time that day.

'Look at me. I'm changing. There's nD tissue growing inside me, Charles. No one knows what is happening to me, why, or what plans they have for me. Maybe the only chance I have of finding out is if we can study one, find out what their flesh is capable of.'

Amanda saw Terrell recoil slightly at the sight of the stigma, but she didn't allow it to upset her. On the contrary, his reaction was all to the good. 'You said they use living things as instruments of their plans,' she went on. 'Maybe there's a bit of the Echo in me, and I swear I will kill myself before I let them use me for an evil purpose. For my sake, my daughter's, all of us – I'm begging you for the one chance we have of stopping what they have in store for us all.'

Amanda finished on this final dramatic note,

feeling emotionally drained. She studied Terrell's eyes, desperately seeking a sign of submission. When it came, she missed it, for Terrell averted his eyes, staring out of the window instead.

'All right, I'll help you as much as I can,' he murmured distantly. 'But in a passive role only. I want no part of your war.'

It was enough. Amanda's body shivered with relief. There was hope again – faint though it may be.

'Thank you, Charles,' she breathed fervently. 'Thank you.'

CHAPTER THIRTEEN

Major General Reece presided over the next war council meeting with a spirit of optimism which had previously been absent. The news of Terrell's decision to co-operate had come like a shot of stimulant in the arm.

'People – we've been on the ropes, but now we're fighting back,' he announced jubilantly. 'We're going to show the nDs they picked the wrong planet and the wrong species this time.'

He turned to face Amanda, seated across the table. 'Look, I don't know how you swung it with Terrell, but you have my gratitude, if not that of every other person at this table.'

The mood was infectious. Amanda grinned. 'Who said I did it for you?' she joked, suddenly light-headed after the bleakest week of her life.

Reece turned to Drake. 'Report?'

Drake stood up. 'General, thanks to Terrell's instructions, we have been able to isolate and dismantle the communications system from the pod and connect it up to a mobile unit. We have already finished conducting test transmissions

– on a short-wave signal which Terrell assures us the nDs can't pick up. In addition, we've assembled a detector which should be able to give advice, warning when a portal is about to form.'

Reece nearly jumped over the desk. 'How much notice?'

Drake looked slightly apologetic. 'Not a lot, I'm afraid sir. Forty, maybe fifty seconds at the most – but it should give that little edge we've been missing. If we're quick off the mark, we can at least be ready for them when they come.'

'So from your point of view, you're almost ready?' Reece enquired.

Drake nodded. 'Basically, we'll be ready when you are, sir. When the time comes, we'll transmit a full-strength signal which will identify Terrell's escape pod, hoping the nDs will come after him.'

Reece nodded with satisfaction. 'Good.' He thought for a moment. 'Bringing the nDs here will place Terrell in direct danger. They don't know what he's told us. All they'll know is that he knows more about them than anyone else. Now that he's helped us, does he wish to be removed to a safer location?'

'No sir. Terrell is fully aware of the dangers and he's prepared to see it through.' Drake paused briefly. 'Sir, with respect, I feel I ought to point out that we may have pegged Terrell wrong. He may be a pacifist, but he's no coward.'

'Point taken,' Reece muttered. He glanced over

at Radcliffe. 'Has that equipment I ordered arrived yet?'

'Everything except the cage, sir – and that's promised within the next two or three hours. The site's all ready, two machine-gun posts in position, as ordered. If anything goes wrong, we'll have them caught in a cross-fire.'

That left only Group Captain Preston to be consulted. Reece addressed her in conjunction with the entire assembly.

'As you are all well aware, this plan to lure and trap an nD is very much a group effort. We've all had some input and we've all had a chance to express our ideas. This is your last chance to also express any reservations you might have, along with any last-minute suggestions.'

Susan Preston didn't bother to stand up. 'The General is very well aware of my personal reservations about this project, they're on record. On its plus side, we may well be able to use this opportunity to test for a toxin that we're working on at the moment with the small amounts of tissue available to us.' She paused, glancing at Amanda. The look spoke volumes. 'However, one last point springs to mind. You've all seen nDs pass through solid walls. What makes any of you think that a mere cage is going to hold them?'

Amanda spoke up. 'We're assuming that once the nDs are cut off from their portals, they're three-dimensional creatures just like us.'

'*Assuming*?' Preston's tone carried a hard overtone.

'A reasonable and sound assumption, given all we've learned about them so far,' Amanda answered.

Preston lapsed into silence, managing to make even that sound like censure in itself.

'All right, so it's a chance we have to take,' Reece snapped. 'Right now we don't have too many other choices.'

He rose to his feet. 'OK, people – so we go in tomorrow. Any last questions before I bring this meeting to a close?'

There was just one. A negative one, and it had to come from Group Captain Preston.

'And what if we fail, General?'

Reece glowered at her. 'Then we'll try again,' he barked testily. 'And if we fail again, we'll try a third time, and a fourth – and again and again until we finally succeed. This is happening *now*. Those people in the village are suffering *now*. We don't have time to sit back and wait for them to make another move. We're going to win this war, Group Captain Preston – because to lose it is utterly unthinkable.'

The trap had been set up in the old hangar, on a suggestion from Terrell that everyone had accepted. His argument – that the signal needed to come from somewhere as close to the Echo escape pod as possible to make it seem authentic – sounded perfectly logical. The fact that the hangar itself would serve as a secondary containment area should anything go wrong was just a bonus.

There was an understandable atmosphere of tension everywhere. People were jumpy, each showing it in different ways. Radcliffe bullied the airmen and, because they understood, they let him do it without their usual banter. Susan Preston, by complete contrast, was unnaturally cheerful and pleasant, smiling at everybody.

Even Reece was not immune. Usually totally authoritative and in command, he seemed edgy and unsure of himself, constantly checking and double-checking the most trivial details.

Right now, for perhaps the tenth time that morning, he was going over the positioning of the cage, suspended by thick steel chains from a complicated series of winches and pulleys attached to the hangar's overhead girders.

'Sure those chains are secure?' he asked Radcliffe.

'Tension monitored by strain gauges,' Radcliffe assured him. 'Tested load capacity of two tonnes.'

'Back-up?'

Radcliffe nodded over to twin sandbagged positions in the two nearest corners of the hangar. 'Two machine-gun emplacements trained on ground zero, sir – as ordered.'

'We've tipped the bullets with our latest test toxin,' Preston told him. 'It seems to be working on Dr Tucker. The wound on her arm looks slightly clearer, although it's too early to be sure at this stage. Blood tests aren't conclusive yet.'

Reece seemed delighted. Welcome words at last. He turned on Drake and Terrell, making final adjustments to the mobile transmitter.

'Everything in order?'

Drake nodded, pointing to an electric cable which snaked across the hangar floor from the transmitter into the cage.

'That lead will carry the transmission into the cage, giving a false point of origin. The nDs will arrive there, not here. Time they figure out we've tricked them it'll be too late. We'll rapidly relocate the cage and isolate it, cutting them off from their portal with no way to get back to it before it closes.'

Reece wasn't sufficiently convinced. 'Let's have a run-through.' He pulled a stopwatch from his pocket, holding it poised. 'Right – go,' he shouted abruptly, catching Radcliffe and his men on the hop.

To their credit, they reacted remarkably quickly.

'Hoist,' Radcliffe shouted.

The chains attached to the cage snapped taut almost immediately. The cage left the ground with a lurch, lifting a good ten feet into the air. Sergeant Tuffley threw a switch on the power winch, and a heavy-duty electric motor whirred into life. The suspended cage began to move across the hangar, swinging wildly.

It lurched to a halt directly above a large isolation chamber on the hangar floor.

'Drop,' Radcliffe yelled.

There was a sharp metallic clang as the release mechanism operated smoothly and efficiently.

The suspended cage, no longer restrained, dropped vertically, straight into the isolation chamber. There was the sudden hiss of pressurised gas.

General Reece hadn't been expecting this. The surprise registered on his face.

Drake grinned at him. 'Little last-minute modification Dr Tucker suggested,' he explained. 'We're pumping an inert gas mixture into the isolation chamber, just in case our atmosphere is too toxic to them. We want one of them alive, not dead.'

Reece looked impressed. 'Good thinking.' He checked his stopwatch before turning to Radcliffe. 'Twelve seconds,' he grunted. 'I want under ten.'

'Sir,' Radcliffe acknowledged, without rancour. He turned to his men, snapping out orders.

'All right, get that cage back into position. Let's run it again.'

The hoist assembly began to wind down from the ceiling. Reece didn't bother to stop and time the second practice, having come to know Radcliffe and trust him. If the operation was humanly possible in less than ten seconds, then Radcliffe would get it down to nine.

He moved on, to where Amanda and Terrell were still making final adjustments to the jury-rigged portal detector. It looked like something out of a Heath Robinson cartoon.

'Success?' he asked.

Amanda looked up, shrugging. 'Unfortunately

there's no way of knowing if it'll work until we put it to the test,' she admitted. 'But if it functions as it should, we will probably get about half a minute of grace.'

Terrell seemed more sure. 'There's every reason to suppose it will work,' he said. 'The Echoes used the core of the equipment to detect black-hole radiation in hyperspace. Dr Tucker seems to think that the nD energy emissions are on a similar wavelength.'

'I've made a few modifications, of course,' Amanda added. 'Besides just detecting, it should now also record for future reference. I'm pretty sure we've got most things covered – audio tape for sound, video for light, sensors in the infra-red and ultra-violet spectrums. Oh, yes – and X-rays set up on a timed sequence,' she added. 'With luck we should get a graphic record of the various stages of portal formation.'

It all sounded pretty impressive. Enough to make General Reece smile, at least temporarily. 'OK, Dr Tucker. But I want you to keep well back from it all. You've been through that hell once already.'

He turned back to Terrell. 'We should be ready to go in about an hour. I'm giving you your last chance to withdraw to safety. The nDs have come after you twice before, and you know more about them than any other man here.'

Terrell shook his head slowly. His face was impassive. 'Thank you, General – but no thanks. It's time to stop running away.' He paused, looking

Reece directly in the eye. 'However, in your own interests, I think you should do everything necessary to prevent them from taking me alive.'

There was a momentary silence as Reece considered these last words, weighing them up, looking for an alternative meaning. There was none. Terrell meant exactly what he had said.

It wasn't something which Reece cared to answer, even acknowledge.

'Right, let's get this show on the road,' he muttered to no one in particular, skirting round the issue.

'Good luck, Charles,' said Amanda, kissing Terrell lightly on the cheek before retreating to the safety zone. 'And thank you.'

They were ready, or at least as ready as one could be for the unknown. Under Radcliffe's relentless bullying, his men had cut their reaction delay to virtually zero, finally arriving at an operation time which was dictated purely by mechanical limitations at nine point five seconds.

With only Drake left beside him, Terrell stood by the transmitter, his finger poised against the switch. He glanced over at Reece, an unspoken question in his eyes.

Reece nodded curtly. 'Switch it on.'

There was a faint hum as Terrell flipped the switch. He fiddled with the tuning dial. 'I'm going to simulate a transmission I might have made to the Echoes, were they still alive. We'll be varying the output characteristic so the nDs can't jam the signal. Even if they don't want to respond, they'll have to come here to shut it down.'

Reece took one last look around, his keen eyes checking everything. He thumbed the button on his field radio, bringing it up to his lips. 'Lock off the hangar,' he ordered, his voice little more than a low croak.

The loud clang of the hangar's huge metal doors launched an unreal, theatrical silence, broken only by the faint hiss of gas from the isolation tank. Radcliffe's men moved slowly and precisely into position against the hangar walls as though they had been choreographed, their assault rifles held at the ready.

The gloom of the closed hangar was suddenly pierced by the beam of a bright spotlight, focused on the suspended cage. It looked for all the world like the set-piece of a stage illusionist, ready for his final show-stopping routine.

Reece was connected in to the PA system now. His voice crackled over the loudspeakers wired up all over the hangar.

'Clear the cage area. Prime weapons. Prepare to transmit signal.'

Drake glanced at Terrell. The man was deathly white, rigid with tension. Although devoid of expression, his face managed to convey unmistakeable fear.

'We can handle them – if they come,' Drake said reassuringly.

Terrell's lips moved. 'They'll come,' he murmured

back. His eyes met Drake's directly, then drifted down to the gun on his hip.

'If they try to take me . . . promise me you won't let them,' he whispered.

It was too heavy. Drake didn't want to handle it. He couldn't think about the possibility of failure, both for Amanda's sake and now Terrell's. He didn't want to be responsible for another man's – another *friend's* – death.

'I told you – we'll take care of them.'

Terrell wasn't convinced. Nor was he willing to let Drake off the hook. 'I want your promise, Drake. You won't let them take me alive.'

Drake glanced away uncomfortably. 'Why me, for Christ's sake?'

'I'd like it to be you.' Terrell forced him to look into his eyes again.

'But I'm the one who got you into this mess.'

Terrell managed a thin smile. 'Then maybe it's poetic justice.'

Reece's voice grated out over the speakers again. 'Prepare to transmit signal in thirty seconds. All units stand by.'

Terrell's finger hovered over the transmitter switch. He caught Drake's eye again. 'Please, Drake. Your promise?' he hissed urgently.

Drake's shoulders drooped with resignation. He stared miserably down at the floor. 'Yes,' he whispered, finally. He hoped to God it wouldn't come to it.

'Transmit,' Reece ordered.

Terrell turned on the transmitter. He thumbed

a button, depressing it for about ten seconds before releasing it.

Drake regarded him in surprise. 'That was it?'

Terrell nodded. 'It's a standard, very compressed signal call. To make it any longer might arouse the nDs' suspicions.' He made a minor adjustment to the tuning dial. 'I'll just take us up in frequency and put it out again.'

Terrell sent the signal a second time then stood back from the transmitter to wait. Nearly a minute passed in absolute silence. Drake's eyes were fixed firmly on the portal detector. There was no sign that it was registering any kind of energy output at all.

The minute stretched out to three, and then five.

Drake's tension had started to amount, making him jumpy. 'What's the matter with the bastards? Why aren't they responding?' he demanded aggressively.

Terrell was more philosophical, merely looking slightly puzzled. He shrugged his shoulders. 'I expect they have their reasons. The nDs always have their reasons.'

He moved back to the transmitter, resetting it. 'I've put it on a spread band, to repeat the signal every fifteen seconds.'

Another five minutes passed, still with no response.

Drake looked round at the others waiting in the safety zone. He could see Amanda, her face

white and contorted with tension. His own edgi-
ness was starting to sink towards depression.
'Maybe they just can't be bothered with us anymore,' he said glumly. 'They've set their little
schemes in motion and they're just going to sit
back and let things happen.'

'Or maybe we're not telling them anything they
don't already know,' Terrell said quietly. 'Perhaps
they're aware that the Echoes are all gone. All
we're telling them is that there is a surviving
Echo spacecraft which is still capable of making a
transmission. They may think we're just experi-
menting with it, sending out signals accidentally.
We may need to say something that they'll really
be interested in.'

Terrell fell silent. Drake eyed him curiously.
'What are you suggesting?' he asked after a
while.

'I should have thought that was obvious. They
know you have my escape vehicle, and they're
obviously not interested in it. What they really
want is *me*. We may need to send them definite
proof that I'm here.'

Drake looked aghast. 'Charles, that's crazy.
We've already said that they might try to take
you. You'd be inviting them to send in a full
assault team with that express purpose.'

Terrell seemed more self-composed now. Or
was it resignation, Drake wondered?

'I don't see that we have any other option,' he
stated, quietly.

'You've got to think about this,' Drake started

to say, but Terrell was already fiddling with the transmitter settings. Drake unclipped his field radio. 'General, we're going to transmit a new signal. This time Terrell is going to identify himself.'

There was a long silence as Reece thought it through. Eventually, his voice crackled out over the speakers again. 'Drake, hold back on that. I'm coming over. Radcliffe, bring in another armed squad from outside the building.'

Reece crossed the hangar floor at the run. He addressed himself directly to Terrell. 'Are you sure about this?'

Terrell's face was grim and determined. 'General, I haven't been so sure about anything for fifty years.'

Reece looked deep into his eyes, admiring the man he saw there. He stood looking at Terrell, silent for a few seconds. Then Terrell nodded towards the transmitter. 'It's already set to send a new signal. Are we ready?'

Reece glanced around the hangar, checking that Radcliffe had moved the additional men into position. 'Ready,' he said curtly.

Terrell fixed Drake with a meaningful look. 'And you, Drake – are you ready?'

The answer came as a faint, almost imperceptible nod. There were a dozen things Drake wanted to say, but his throat seemed to have locked up.

It was enough to tell Terrell what he wanted to know. He moved back to the transmitter again.

'Transmitting now,' he muttered calmly, and depressed the call button.

Drake's eyes were glued back on the make-shift detector as the seconds ticked away. A small red bulb glowed faintly, showing that the thing was at least powered up. Then one of the dials flickered into life, its needle making three erratic little jumps and finally whirring off the scale.

A pulsing audio bleep started up, rising in pitch and frequency until it was an almost continuous electronic whistle.

Drake felt his guts tighten. There was a brief surge of elation before the fear beneath it fully registered. 'It works,' he blurted out. 'This is it, they're coming !' Along with everyone else inside the hangar, his eyes flickered towards the illuminated cage.

The detector signal had risen to an ear-splitting scream. 'Can't you shut that damned thing off?' Reece shouted.

Drake flipped a switch. In the abrupt silence which followed, there was only the sharp metallic clicking of weapons being cocked.

'Hold your fire. Await orders,' Reece bellowed. The silence descended once again.

The geometric lines of the cage were beginning to distort. It seemed to bulge outward, momentarily becoming a globe rather than a cuboid. The spotlight bathing it appeared to pale, as a greater radiance developed inside its beam, radiating outwards like a sun-going supernova. The crackle of unrestrained energy built inside the hangar, echoing off the walls.

The cage itself was no longer visible now, other than as a blinding sphere of light. But something dark was already forming inside it, flickering, changing shape, expanding.

Before it had form, it had voice. The voice of a wild beast, realising itself to be trapped. The suspended cage began to shake and rattle violently as the thing materialising inside it tore and raged at its confining bars. A roar of pure, savage fury exploded out into the hangar, making the metal walls rattle.

The cage began to move, out of the portal. The rapidly changing shapes inside it started to coalesce into a single dark mass, forming a single shape.

The thing was big – much bigger than anyone had imagined. Squat, wide, powerful – it was clearly alien, clearly inhuman. Yet it was recognisable, if only as something out of dim racial memory and nightmares. Momentarily, everyone inside the hangar saw their individual personification of every ogre, goblin, troll and demon in human legend and folk lore.

So it's not been just fifty years, Reece thought, in a strange moment of clarity. The war with the nDs was older than time, as old as Earth itself.

It was a realisation which carried an overriding sense of resignation, yet it carried hope, too. Even in the dark ages, Man had managed to keep the nDs at bay, just one step short of destroying him and his world. And always the nDs had persisted, never flagging in their attack. But now Man had science and technology, the first glimmerings of understanding. The war with the nDs *would* go on, perhaps for countless years – but Man would eventually win, because it was in his nature and destiny to do so.

All this flashed through Reece's mind in an instant, like a dream which was almost as quickly forgotten. He snapped back to reality, the present moment.

The trapped nD was still roaring with fury, still raging inside its confinement with unbelievable speed, power and agility. The metal bars of the cage were beginning to bend and snap like willow twigs.

'Release the cage!' Reece bellowed, realising that the creature would be free at any moment.

The cage dropped towards the isolation chamber, taking the nD with it. There was a brief moment when Reece dared to think he might allow himself to breathe again.

It was not to be.

Radcliffe's voice rose above the din in a scream of panic. 'It's breaking out! We can't contain it.'

The isolation chamber was disintegrating, being ripped apart from the inside as though it were made of papier mâché. Even as Reece watched hopelessly, the nD was beginning to emerge, tossing great pieces of destroyed equipment aside with incredible energy and power.

'Open fire,' Reece yelled. 'Don't let it make it back to the portal.'

The two machine gun nests opened up in a withering crossfire. The nD hardly seemed to notice the hail of bullets, moving towards the still-open portal where the cage had been. Just at the last moment, it seemed to slow up, stagger and falter in its inexorable progress. Then it lurched forward once again, fell into the swirling distortion and was gone.

The portal closed abruptly. There was a sudden, terrible silence which seemed to go on for ever.

Everyone gaped at the scene of devastation the nD had left behind it. Reece found his voice first.

'We've taken a bad hit, but we've learned a lesson,' he announced. 'We may have failed this time, but they'll be back, and next time we'll be ready for them.'

He turned to Terrell. 'You see, we just have to go on fighting – and believing we can win,' he added, in a much quieter voice. 'Every time we try and fail, we're one step nearer to trying and winning. We owe it to the world to carry on.'

Terrell nodded. 'Yes, General. I think I understand you now.' He looked over at Drake. 'They'll still try to take your world, Drake. Those people in the village – Amanda, her little girl – the world – it's up to you now. You mustn't let them.'

'Charles, *we* won't let them,' Drake corrected.

There was a sad, distant but resigned smile on Terrell's face. 'Not me, Drake. The nDs are aware

I'm here now, and I know too much. They'll come for me again, and they'll take me. It's your fight now.'

The man seemed perfectly composed, Drake thought – yet he appeared to be trembling violently, his whole body shaking. It was slightly unnerving.

Too late, he suddenly realised that Terrell wasn't shaking at all. It was the air immediately around his body which was moving, shimmering like a heat haze.

'No!' wailed Drake. 'Charles – no!'

The portal seemed to open up inside Terrell's stomach, pulling in his body like a spindled paper cut-out. Drake snatched out at his hand, trying to grasp it and pull him back, but his fingers closed around thin air. Reece grabbed at his shoulder, pulling him away from the rapidly expanding portal.

Terrell's legs had folded up underneath him, and were being sucked into the void like jelly through a straw. His torso, shoulders and head appeared to float in mid-air. His face was strangely calm.

'You promised, Drake,' he said quietly.

Drake nodded. Not many of us get the chance to make the ultimate sacrifice more than once in our lives, he thought. Not many of us ever choose to make it. Terrell had already made it once when he left Earth to look for lasting peace and he was making it again now. Drake understood. It was his war now. They would fight it with biological weapons, military technology, solidarity.

He knew what his role was.

His hand dropped to the service Webley on his hip, pulling it smoothly from its holster.

'We'll fight them, Charles,' he vowed softly, then shot Terrell neatly between the eyes.

Pasiphae

William Smethurst

PASIPHAE is the most advanced military communications satellite ever built. But strange signals are penetrating its security system – signals that appear to emanate from the fourteenth century. And as chaos strikes the world's communications systems from Paris to Tokyo, it becomes obvious that the enigmatic messages are full of murderous passion.

The key lies in the mind of a young archaeologist in Herefordshire who finds herself drawn to the tomb of a Franklin, dead for five hundred years. Night after night, she feels herself compelled to lie by his effigy, haunted by dreams of love and betrayal. Lizzie Draude has become a carrier, a transmitter between the time of Richard II and the present-day world. But can the flow of signals be stopped before horrendous forces are unleashed, destroying more than Lizzie herself?

'Enthralling' *The Times*

0 7472 4817 6

Ibryen

Roger Taylor

Count Ibryen has been driven from his ancestral land by the Gevethen – strange and powerful usurpers. He and his loyal followers have taken refuge in the mountains, and are fighting a relentless but failing guerilla war.

Then a mysterious call lures Ibryen away from his followers. Together with Rachyl and the enigmatic Traveller, he goes in search of an answer to the desperate need in that call, and in the hope of finding another way to oppose the Gevethen's awful power.

But his journey leads him into worlds he could not even have imagined . . . And to knowledge of a power within himself, of strange cloud-lands, and of the dark presence that even the Gevethen bend the knee to.

But what will this knowledge avail him against the Gevethen's might, now gathering for a final crushing blow against his stronghold while he is absent?

0 7472 5007 3

HEADLINE FEATURE